Several rounds from a high-powered rifle rent the air. "Take cover."

Zane hit the accelerator, bounced across the shallow ditch and then slammed on the brakes.

Bliss was on the side of the shooter, but she already had her gun ready and the window down.

He got out, keeping his head low, and moved behind the bed of his truck. Distant lightning gave just enough light to see someone running through the woods. The man shot again.

Squeezing the trigger, Zane returned fire.

Bliss shot two rounds.

She asked quietly, "Do you see the gunman?"

"No." He continued to look for movement but saw nothing. "I'm going to check if the man's been hit."

"I've got your back."

"Stay here." He crossed the ditch and entered the thick woods.

Movement came from behind him. "I asked you to stay there."

"You asked for my help, and I told you I'd be your backup."

Connie Queen has spent her life in Texas, where she met and married her high school sweetheart. Together they've raised eight children and are enjoying their grandchildren. Today, as an empty nester, Connie lives with her husband and her Great Dane, Nash, and is working on her next suspense novel.

Books by Connie Queen

Love Inspired Suspense

Justice Undercover
Texas Christmas Revenge
Canyon Survival
Abduction Cold Case
Tracking the Tiny Target
Rescuing the Stolen Child

Visit the Author Profile page at LoveInspired.com.

RESCUING THE STOLEN CHILD

CONNIE QUEEN

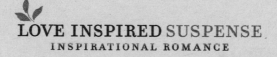

LOVE INSPIRED SUSPENSE

INSPIRATIONAL ROMANCE

LOVE INSPIRED® SUSPENSE
INSPIRATIONAL ROMANCE

ISBN-13: 978-1-335-59766-3

Rescuing the Stolen Child

Love Inspired
22 Adelaide St. West, 41st Floor
Toronto, Ontario M5H 4E3, Canada
www.LoveInspired.com

Printed in U.S.A.

It were better for him that a millstone were hanged
about his neck, and he cast into the sea,
than that he should offend one of these little ones.
—*Luke* 17:2

I'd like to dedicate this book to my devoted readers.
It's truly humbling to hear friends from church,
those I went to school with, neighbors
and my relatives say they read my book.
It tickles me and makes me at a loss for words. From my
nine-year-old granddaughter to ninety-two-year-old Floyd—
and everyone in between—thank you!

ONE

As soon as Texas Ranger Zane Adcock walked through the door and heard Sugar barking, he knew something wasn't right. His seven-year-old Maltese always greeted him in a flurry of excitement and yapping.

"Sugar..." His gaze quickly took in the dark house. Occasional streaks of lightning illuminated the space, and long shadows enveloped the room. His leather boots clomped on the wooden floor as he strode toward the back of the home. The canine bundle of energy must've gotten herself trapped somewhere. Being small, it was easy for her to get into some unusual predicaments. When she was just a pup, she'd somehow gotten stuck under a laundry basket, and he wondered if it had happened again.

The Maltese continued to bark with agitation, drowning out the rain that pinged the roof.

"Sugar. Where are you, baby?" He entered his bedroom and flipped on the light. The dog was nowhere in sight. A thumping came from the closet, and he opened the door. Sugar leaped into his arms, shivering.

"What's wrong?" A bad feeling washed over him. He glanced around. He'd left her in her crate this morning. Faye, his housekeeper, normally let her into the backyard while she cleaned but returned her to the pen before she left for the day. Maybe Faye forgot to return her to her pen. *But Faye never forgets.*

Sugar licked his face repeatedly.

"Okay. Okay." He chuckled. "I'm here." He was glad to see Sugar was all right, but the hair rose on his arms. He glanced around the room, his gaze taking in his surroundings. The bed had been made, and the hamper that had been overflowing this morning was empty. Nothing appeared out of place. The bathroom door was shut, but a light shone from underneath. Faye was a stickler for conserving electricity and always turned off all the lights.

"Get down," he whispered and returned Sugar to the floor. He removed his pistol from the back of his waistband and swung the door wide. It slammed into the bathtub, bouncing partway shut.

His gaze fell to a bloody knife on the counter.

Sugar launched into a yapping tirade as a creak came from behind him.

Before Zane spun, someone shoved a cloth bag over his head, and something cold and hard jabbed into his side. The unmistakable click of a trigger followed.

"Drop your weapon."

Zane's mind scrambled as his hand gripped the handle. As tempting as it was to try to disarm the man, no doubt the barrel of a gun prodding him in the middle would go off.

"Don't even think about it, Lieutenant Zane Adcock. Drop it now if you want to see your loved ones again."

The unfamiliar raspy voice boldly pronounced every

word, alerting him the intruder wanted Zane to know he knew him. This was no random break-in. *Loved ones?*

The man could've already killed him if that was his plan. With Zane's back to the guy, he released his grip, and his gun tumbled to his feet.

The cloth bag restricted his breathing, but light filtered through the thin fabric. Sugar continued to jump and yap, hitting his leg. In the mirror, the dark silhouette of a man hovered behind him, but Zane couldn't make out the details. "What do you want?"

"Pretty easy to plant evidence, ain't it?"

It took only a moment for the comment to sink in. Zane had never planted evidence in his life, but he remained silent. He eased forward, if only an inch— anything to distance himself from the weapon. A split second was all he needed to drop to the ground, sweep out with his leg, bring the man down and retrieve his gun. Hopefully without getting shot.

The metal dug deeper into his side. "Listen carefully."

A clicking noise that sounded like that of an old recorder was followed by a child's cry. "Grandpa," said a boy's voice. "This is Wyatt."

Zane froze. *Grandpa?* Sage, his only daughter, had moved away several years ago, and they hadn't spoken since. Sage left months after her mother's tragic death. She had a son? Zane's throat parched as he suddenly had to swallow. He listened intently.

"I want to go home..." More sobbing and then a clacking sound as the recording stopped.

His muscles tremored as anger rose inside of him, threatening to bubble over. Did he dare try to overtake this man? If he knocked the kidnapper out of commission, would the Texas Rangers be able to find his grandson?

For a second, the metal disappeared from Zane's side before a sharp point replaced it. A knife. The blade poked through his Western shirt, and the tip pierced his skin, sending a biting sting down his side. Warm fluid trickled down.

The intruder's other hand tugged the cloth hard, snapping Zane's head back, and the blade went to his throat. "Listen very carefully, Lieutenant. The red stain on the knife is paint, not your four-year-old grandson's blood. But it will be the lad's if you fail. You helped work a case sixteen years ago involving Sean Weaver. Someone in the police department set him up." Hot, angry breath sifted through the hood onto the side of Zane's neck. "Sean's no cop killer. Someone shot my brother and planted evidence, and now he's scheduled for execution. The Rangers assisted in that case. If you want to see the boy alive, find who framed him, and clear my brother. You only have until Friday at midnight."

With a jerk, the man yanked him backward, causing his knee to hyperextend. The instantaneous agony caused him to hunch forward, and the man slammed Zane's forehead into the bathroom counter. Pain exploded, and he stumbled to keep his balance.

The sound of running feet and then a door banging.

Sugar yapped and jumped on him.

Ripping the cloth bag from his head, Zane retrieved his weapon from the floor and ran for the back door. Wooziness caused him to stagger, but he managed to race through the house. He swung the door open in time to see an older Chevrolet pickup peel out of his driveway. It was too dark and rainy to make out the color or the license plate, but the shape gave the model away.

Quickly, he scrambled for his phone and called the Texas Rangers' office. As soon as he was done relaying what had happened, he scrolled through his contacts and hit another number.

As the phone rang, he wondered how he was going to explain about his grandson—a child he never knew existed. Where was Sage? Did she know Wyatt was missing?

Not only did he lose contact with his only child several years ago, but now his grandson was kidnapped because of him. This would win him no favors with his daughter.

Sweat trickled down Bliss Walker's face like an irritating spiderweb, begging to be swiped away, but she ignored the impulse. Moist night air had the room sweltering, and the sound of rain hitting the windows should've been soothing, but it wasn't. Temptation to halt her workout long enough to turn down the thermostat on the air-conditioning enticed her, but she shoved it to the back of her mind. She could do this.

Her heart raced, and her loud pants for breath told her she couldn't last much longer. Determination nipped her psyche.

A glance at the monitor showed she'd been on the torture machine for fifty-eight minutes. Less than two more to go.

With a yank on the handle, the row machine's seat slid back in chaotic rhythm. Her energy waned even as she dug deeper for one more rep. And then another. Anger pushed her.

Tears burned her eyes.

I'm sorry, Adam. I let you down. Let us both down.

She'd answered that dreaded call years ago when Adam's Nissan Altima had wrecked and was sitting on the side of the road, but her husband and son were missing. Her husband's body had been discovered six hours later, but not their five-year-old son. Standing over Adam's grave, she promised not to stop searching for Mitchell until she'd found him safe.

Eleven weeks ago, a hiker had come across Mitchell's remains in the woods less than eight miles from where the Altima had wrecked.

Mitchell wasn't coming home. Hope was gone. How could she have spent the last fourteen years failing her one and only mission? Find her missing son and bring him home. It was all that had mattered. What she lived for.

Her muscles pleaded with her to stop, but she pushed harder.

Thirty-three more seconds. Thirty-two...

The framed photograph of Bliss accepting the keys to the city—an award given to her organization for finding a truckload of twenty-four kids being transported across North Texas before crossing state lines—seemed to mock her. The Bring the Children Home Project had been the perfect way to channel her efforts of finding Mitchell. She'd make a difference. She'd left her career as a deputy US marshal to create the group of highly trained volunteers.

Twenty-one seconds. Twenty...

"I can never repay you, ma'am. After thirteen years, you found my precious Cindy." Mrs. Monk's tearful gratitude had helped Bliss believe. Believe in herself.

Believe children could be found no matter how much time had passed.

Nine seconds. Eight seconds.

God, if you grant me this one thing, I'll do all that I can to help families. I'll be a light to others.

Ding.

The handle flung out of her hands, the cable snapping back into place. She buried her face in her palms and burst into tears.

Why?

The unanswered question plagued her.

She grabbed her water bottle from the cup holder and took a long swig. When she got up from the row machine, her muscles tightened like a pair of jeans two sizes too small, letting her know she'd pushed it too hard. Again.

Exercise had become a form of punishment. Daily workouts used to bring her enjoyment, endorphins that reenergized her for another day. She needed to take care of herself since she wasn't getting younger. Would she ever find meaning in life again? She'd always been an optimist. The thought of not bouncing back scared her.

She grabbed the towel from the arm of the suede chair and wiped her face and arms. A long cold shower was calling her name.

On the way to her bedroom from her gym-office combo, she stepped into her living room just as her cell phone vibrated on the end table. Whoever was calling this late would have to try again tomorrow. She was in no mood for conversation. Not tonight. Not on the fourteenth anniversary of the worst day of her life.

Curious, she glanced at the screen anyway. Caller Unknown. Good. At least it wasn't one of her team members. She punched the Decline button, but before she took two steps, the phone vibrated again. With a grumble, she snapped, "Hello."

"Bliss. I need your help."

Her defenses fell. Even without identifying himself, she recognized the lieutenant's deep voice immediately. Zane would never call if it wasn't important, especially this late. Someone at the office must've given him her cell phone number. Zane had never reached out since she'd broken off their engagement after college almost twenty-five years ago. Every year or two, they'd pass one another if working on the same case, but it had been all business. "What can I do for you, Lieutenant?"

"I need you to find a missing boy for me."

"I'm sorry—you must not have heard." Her heart constricted, but she had to get used to saying no. "I'm retiring from the Bring the Children Home Project."

A long silence greeted her, and the awkwardness grew. She cleared her throat. "I'm turning the reins over to Riggs and Annie Brenner. Friday is my last day. If you need additional help, Josie Hunt will be taking—"

"I need *you*." His voice sounded strained, almost pleading. So unlike him.

"I'm sorry, Zane." She had to stick to her plan. If she continued taking cases, she'd never leave the organization. There was always a child in trouble, a family in pain. And her heart couldn't take another loss.

The last couple of months, she'd been running on autopilot and making mistakes. A donation she'd forgotten to deposit. She'd confused the names of the Bensons' daughter with that of the Stevensons' while updating the parents, and she'd failed to remember a safety class she was supposed to teach at Liberty Elementary School.

Not anything that had cost a case, but careless just the same, which was so unlike her. Let someone else deal with the emotional aches and longing. Bliss simply had nothing left to give.

But she'd always respected Zane and his work, even after they'd gone their separate ways. This investigation must be important, or he wouldn't have called. "Is there something that makes this case significant?"

"My four-year-old grandson has been kidnapped."

The words thrust like a dagger to her heart. "I didn't know you had grandkids."

"Please, Bliss. You're the best. The Texas Rangers will work the case, and we're good at apprehending bad guys. But no one is better than you at finding children."

Unless it was her own. Heaviness weighed on her chest. Zane had no idea what he was asking of her. She wasn't at the top of her game anymore. And to have the lieutenant depending on her... What if she let him down? What if, at a critical moment, she made a mistake?

Against her better judgment, she uttered, "I'll agree to talk with you. I make no promises. Where are you?"

"At the end of your driveway. At the gate. Want to let me in?"

She moved to the window and glanced out. Sure enough, there were truck headlights reflecting off the rain along the side of her road. How had he known she'd moved to her parents' old homeplace? She hit the app on her phone. "It's open."

She hustled to her bedroom and changed out of her workout clothes and into a pair of khaki pants and a polo shirt. A glance in the mirror made her thankful for waterproof mascara. Maybe she should let Chandler and Annie from the team work with Zane instead of her personally. She could manage things from the office and wouldn't worry about making a costly blunder. That was it. She would just oversee the search.

The doorbell rang.

She padded through the house and opened the door. Zane's large frame swallowed the entrance. Dressed in his Texas Ranger attire of a white Western shirt, a navy tie, jeans and boots, one could easily detect the authority in his presence.

Rain dripped from his Stetson, and he removed it. "Thank you for seeing me."

A tinge of salt and pepper lined his military-style haircut, adding to the experienced lawman's appearance.

"Come in." She turned and walked into the living room. The lieutenant had always been a handsome man, but at forty-five years old—just two years older than herself—he had a more solid, tough look she found even more attractive than his younger lanky self.

A bluish-gray line ran down his forehead, and dried blood streaked above his eyebrow. His gaze connected with hers. A storm of emotions danced in his brown eyes. Turning him away was going to be one of the hardest things she'd ever done.

"I knew I could count on you."

Oh, he played dirty. "Like I said, we have a good team. Annie and Riggs are in West Texas, and it will take them a few hours to get here."

"I can't wait." Zane shook his head. "We only have until Friday at midnight, which gives us less than four days. Then the kidnapper is going to kill the boy. We must move now."

TWO

Zane ignored the pounding of his head. It irked him that he hadn't prevented the attack. Now he was left with no choice but to beg assistance from his ex-fiancée from years ago.

"Have a seat." She indicated the white sofa with a sweep of her hand.

"I'd rather stand." A glance around the place showed Bliss hadn't lost her style. The tall ceilings and the stone fireplace gave the room a welcoming feel. Even though the leather couch fit its owner with a touch of class, he sensed he'd get it all dirty and ruin it.

"Suit yourself. Tell me what happened."

"Can we talk while on the road?"

She shot him a slight smile. "I know you're ready to search now, but you realize it's better to have a plan than hope to find the child by blindly looking."

"We identified the kidnapper." He noted Bliss's eyebrows lifted, showing her surprise. "The man told me he was Sean Weaver's brother. Sean is sitting on death row for killing a Liberty police officer and is scheduled for execution on Friday. If Sean is exonerated by then, his brother will not kill my grandson."

"Friday. Hence the four-day deadline."

"Exactly. The Texas Rangers helped work the Weaver case, and the kidnapper is using the boy as leverage to get us to look into the old case. One call to Chasity Spears, our investigator with the Rangers, and she's already gotten back with me. Lawrence Weaver is our suspect. Sixty-two-year-old factory worker who's been with his last job for thirty-one years." He held up his cell phone with the image of Lawrence's driver's license photo pulled up. "Chasity is checking to make certain we have the current address right now."

"That's an immense help."

He explained about Lawrence waiting for him when he came home tonight and then the recording of his grandson's voice.

"Do you have a recent photo and description of what your grandson was wearing?"

Zane knew she would need to ask these questions, but he had little to go on. "Not yet. Chasity is working on it. His name is Wyatt and he's four. That's all I know."

Her expressive brown eyes continued not to show what she was thinking. Something she'd always been good at. "Where was the last place he was seen?"

"I don't know. I haven't talked with my daughter, Sage, yet."

"Why not?" Her voice remained neutral and non-judgmental.

"I don't have her contact information." He ran his hand through his hair and instantly regretted it when he bumped the knot on his forehead. Did he need to admit the truth to Bliss? Would she think he was a bad dad? Of course that was what she'd conclude. He needed to be honest. Finding Wyatt was more important than his pride. "I haven't talked with her since she turned eighteen. Sage made it clear she didn't want me in her life. I learned I had a grandson only tonight."

"I'm sorry." Compassion crossed the former marshal's expression, and he hated it. Anger or hatefulness was easier to stomach than sympathy.

I wish you were the one killed in that car wreck. I hate you! His daughter's last words had stung to the core, but he had believed the feelings were temporary. He'd hoped she would've reached out a long time ago.

A ding indicated a text had come through. He glanced at his cell phone and then shoved it into his back pocket. "I have Lawrence Weaver's address, and the judge signed off on a warrant to search his place. It's a little over an hour from here. Are you ready to go?"

She shot him a look that he didn't understand.

"What? What's wrong?"

"I can't do this, Zane." She sighed. "Chandler and Annie are taking the cases now. Riggs, Annie's husband, is also on our team. They're a few hours away from Liberty but can be here by morning. We have capable volunteers. Chandler and his search-and-rescue bloodhound are great at tracking. I'll contact everyone, and by sunup, they should be here."

Bliss couldn't do this to him. Anger bit at him. "There's a scared four-year-old boy out there somewhere in the hands of a violent kidnapper. You're turning your back on him?"

Pain danced in her eyes and his irritation subsided. She'd just learned about her son.

Calm down, Adcock. This is not her fault. He took a step toward her. "I'm sorry about your boy. I can't imagine what it must be like for you. I'm sure your team would be helpful. But, please, I'd feel more confident if you were leading them."

She stared at him. More awkward seconds ticked by. Finally, she said, "Please don't try imagining what it's like. I wouldn't want anyone to understand. Let's go."

What could he say to that? He decided it was best not to respond and be thankful she had agreed.

She held up a finger in the air. "I'm only going with you until Annie and Riggs get here. Then I'll oversee the investigation from my office. There's a lot of information to gather. A recent photo. The location of the abduction. Something with the victim's scent for the search-and-rescue team to use. We also need to learn connections and properties of the suspect."

Inwardly, he sighed. They had work to do. "I understand."

A few minutes later, they were in his truck and pulling out of her driveway. As the rain continued to pour, Bliss texted on her phone. He assumed she was sending messages to her team.

Even though Bliss hadn't wanted to help, Zane was glad she had come with him. Except for the worry lines across her forehead, she had changed little in the years he'd known her, and she looked just as athletic as she had when they were dating. He couldn't say the same for himself.

Not having family close, Zane spent the majority of his waking hours at work and with his coworkers. But most of them had families at home or a person they dated. In times when something more personal was going on, he wished he had someone in his corner, whether it be his daughter or someone else. Maybe that was why he had pressured Bliss to assist him. He needed more than a capable officer. He needed a friend.

If Lawrence had brought Wyatt to his house, this could all be over within the hour. The sounds of the boy's voice kept replaying through his mind. *Grandpa. This is Wyatt.* Had Sage told her son about him?

He could only imagine how that conversation would've gone. The idea of him being a grandpa was surreal.

A ding sounded, and Bliss looked at her phone. "Annie and Riggs are both sick and will not be able to come for a couple of days. Josie and Chandler are en route."

"Thanks." A glance at the former US marshal showed her looking out of the window, her back as stiff as a piece of Uncle Emmett's beef jerky after sitting in the sun for a day. Inwardly, he sighed again. He shouldn't have asked Bliss to help find Wyatt. News traveled fast through law departments, and he'd heard about her son within a couple of days of his discovery. She had suffered enough loss. He'd meant to reach out to her and had even bought a sympathy card, but the sentiment had seemed inadequate, and he'd never mailed it.

But he had bigger problems than thinking about how he should've offered comfort.

Like how he was going to keep her and his grandson safe if they found the kidnapper.

Bliss squeezed the door handle as they pulled into the drive. It was still an hour before sunup, and the rain had slowed to a drizzle. The headlights reflected off the puddles left by last night's storms, promising another sweltering day. She prayed the boy was kept indoors and not in the elements. The chances were slim Lawrence would keep his kidnapped victim at his home or leave clues to where he had taken him. But sometimes criminals didn't think things through before acting.

"Ranger Dryden will be here in an hour with a drone to search the surrounding area, and Ranger Randolph is looking up the Liberty police investigator who worked Sean Weaver's case."

"I remember them well. Excellent officers."

Zane turned to her. "Do you need to wait for your team?"

"A Texas Ranger counts as backup." She offered a slight smile. "Every minute counts, so let's go in."

He parked in the circular rock drive. The house was dark, and Zane left his headlights on.

Please, God, help us find something that leads us to the boy. The silent prayer made her feel a little better. While she was busy with being a US marshal, talking to God had been an occasional occurrence until her husband and son had gone missing. Then she had started praying multiple times per day, and her faith grew as well as participating in church. She also reached out to others and became more comfortable offering encouraging words—something that had always made her feel awkward before. After learning Mitchell's remains had been discovered, the devastation had tempted her to quit praying and had for almost a week. But who else could she talk to if not God? Regretfully, the action had become robotic to her, but she didn't want her faith to suffer, so she kept trying and hoped the close feelings would return.

The brick home perched in a clump of trees, and an older car was parked under a carport. A pot of pink and yellow zinnias sat beside the front door, and a wind chime with a large Texas star clanged noisily in the breeze. Besides the grass needing to be mowed, the place didn't look as neglected as she had imagined. Thankfully, no dog came out to greet them.

Zane turned to her. "Wait here until I clear the house?"

"I'm no longer a deputy US marshal, but I still know how to use a gun. My thirty-eight is ready." She patted her leg, indicating an ankle holster.

His gaze narrowed. "You're right. Come on."

"I've got the back door."

At his nod, she stepped out of the truck onto gravel. While Zane approached the front door, she flanked him to the side of the house and to the back corner. Darkness encompassed her. Even after giving her eyes time to adjust, she couldn't see well. It forced her to use the flashlight from her belt.

She heard a rapping on the door.

"This is Texas Ranger Zane Adcock. I need to talk with you. I have a search warrant."

She knew he didn't expect Lawrence to answer, but the formality was more for if there were other persons in the home.

A shed sat in the backyard with the door ajar, and she kept her eyes on it for movement. Dark, secluded buildings or areas of the residence that no one could hear a child were the obvious places to hide someone.

There was another knock.

Bliss half expected some kind of commotion, but there was only silence followed by the lieutenant moving through the home and identifying himself. A minute later, the back door swung wide. Zane stood in the opening. "Clear."

She pointed toward the backyard. "There's a shed I want to check out."

"I'll go with you." He bounded off the porch and caught up to her as she rounded the corner of the house.

Her heart picked up the pace, and she held her pistol ready. Zane removed the flashlight from his belt, and his gaze met hers. They nodded at each other at the same time. With the ranger on her heels, she stepped in first. Both of them quickly took in the eight-by-twelve-foot shed. A push mower sat in the middle of the space, and a variety of tools and car parts cluttered the perimeter.

He said, "Clear."

She dropped her weapon to her side, disappointment slamming into her. She knew the chances were slim, but she couldn't help getting her hopes up. "I'll assist you in searching the house for evidence after I look around a bit more in here."

Zane nodded. "I'm going to see if I can find anything that leads us to where he may have taken the boy."

After he strode back to the house, she took her time surveying the shed, looking for signs of a typical kidnapping—duct tape, rope, candy and toys. She didn't see any of those items, but they could be in the man's truck or home.

From what Zane had said, Lawrence Weaver had moved quickly. The chance he brought his young victim back here to his own land that he knew well, at least for a bit, was iffy. Maybe fifty-fifty. The man may have left the child in his truck while he was inside Zane's house, or he could've stashed him away somewhere.

When she stepped outside a few minutes later, her cell phone rang. It was Chandler, asking her if she had found anything that belonged to the victim.

"Not yet, but we're still searching. Hopefully, Zane will be in touch with his daughter soon and can be supplied an item. I appreciate your help, Chandler." She clicked off and headed for the house.

As she walked in, she noted the outdated paneling had been painted white, giving it a fresh look. Zane sat behind a desk piled with mail and documents. "Was Lawrence married?"

"No. Looks like his wife died three years ago due to kidney failure. You need to see this." Zane pointed to a stack of papers and frowned. "I've got some bad news."

She inhaled and moved closer. "What is it?"

He held up a pile of papers. "These bills go back at least four years."

Bliss raised her eyebrow.

"Our man has been fighting liver cancer. The last treatment is dated three weeks ago."

She didn't say a word but understood the implications. The kidnapper had nothing to lose. His wife was dead, and he was dying. It didn't matter if he lived or died. His final purpose in life was to save his brother from execution.

This put Wyatt in a whole new danger.

"I'm sorry." She offered no explanation.

Zane's jaw twitched.

"If you want to keep digging and see if you can find where he brought Wyatt, that would help. Chandler called me a few minutes ago, asking if we have anything that would have the boy's scent. Have you heard back on the whereabouts of your daughter?"

"Not yet. I just checked in with Chasity. There was a child abduction yesterday in Pascal, three hours east of here near the Louisiana border. The mom was on her way to her car at a grocery store and tried to stop the kidnapper. The mom was dragged by the vehicle. Chasity is in contact with the local police there and should have more information shortly on the identity of the victim."

Zane's voice remained neutral, but Bliss could tell by the red creeping up the back of his neck he wasn't happy. Her heart went out to him, but the best thing she could do was help find Wyatt with the intel they had. She progressed slowly through the house, taking in everything that would show signs the boy had been here. If so, they wouldn't have to wait to talk to Zane's daughter.

While the lieutenant concentrated his efforts on the paperwork, she moved to the back of the home. A slight lip crossed the threshold of the hallway. Instead of paneling, the walls were constructed of Sheetrock, and the ceiling was at least a foot taller. This area looked like a newer addition. The first bedroom she came to contained a library of books of mainly old romance novels and a few travel magazines. She slid on a pair of plastic gloves so as not to contaminate evidence and sifted through them. A sewing machine, complete with a wooden cabinet, sat against the opposite wall. Her mom used to have one just like that, and Bliss remembered she and her sister would get matching dresses for Easter every year. A glance in the closet showed stacks of material and a couple of hand-pieced quilts.

There was nothing to indicate a child had been kept here.

The clomp of boots on tile carried through the house, telling her Zane was switching to a different room.

Bliss moved to the main bedroom, presumably Lawrence's. The neatly made bed caused her to wonder if he had been in the military. A chest of drawers blocked a door leading to the outside, and a nightstand butted against the bed. Again, she searched through drawers to see if there was anything that would lead them to the kidnapped boy, but nothing appeared useful.

She looked at the closet door and noted it was larger than the others in the house. Cloth baskets neatly sat lined on a shelf on the right, and a narrow rod held a few clothes on the left. The room was open and free of clutter.

That was odd. The floor was raised.

Was that a door in the closet floor?

Due to climate and soil, rarely did houses in North Texas have a basement. And this one would not be easy to access. Maybe it was some sort of safe room.

Her heart raced, as this would be the perfect place to keep a child. "Zane," she called. "I may have found something."

There wasn't a handle, but the door was thick and framed with one-by-four-inch boards. She leaned over and tugged upward on the corner. It was much heavier than expected, and she let it back down. Widening her stance for better leverage, she grabbed the side again and heaved.

With a creak, the door opened a couple of inches before it caught like something held it. One quick jerk, and it pulled free. She leaned the door against the shelves.

A cotton string swung freely, and something clinked down the steps. Quickly, she shone her flashlight into the opening. A deep hole with metal stairs. It looked like an old storm cellar. Maybe Lawrence or the previous owner had built the new addition over the shelter.

Bliss yelled, "Wyatt, are you down there?"

She took two quick steps down when she glanced at where the string had been attached. Staring back at her was a grenade duct-taped to the wall.

The pin was missing. That must've been what had fallen.

Her heart stuttered. Not having time to see if Wyatt was in the cellar, she had no choice but to get rid of the explosive before it went off, possibly hurting the boy and her.

She yanked the grenade from the tape and dashed up the steps to the main floor while being careful not to shake too much. Zane strode down the hall toward her. She spun on her heel and held the bomb at arm's length. Blood thumped through her ears.

"What did you find?" Zane moved into the room.

"Stay out of my way," she squealed and skirted around him.

"Drop it and run."

"No. Wyatt may be down there." The chest blocked the bedroom door. "Move the drawers!"

The furniture crashed to the floor as Zane threw it and then swung the door open. It couldn't last another second or two. Shaking uncontrollably, she darted outside.

A metal stock tank was about twenty feet away. She sprinted, and her foot stepped into a hole, causing her to stumble. In a motion of pure desperation, she flung the grenade toward the water trough. Just as she let go, she was tackled from behind.

Boom!

Water flew into the air like the winning jump of a cannonball contest, and bits of metal showered the ground.

The pressure on her back made it impossible to catch her breath. She wiggled. "Get off me."

He rolled away and pushed onto his knees. "Are you all right? Were you hurt?"

Her head snapped around at him as she dusted herself off. "My ears are ringing, but I think I'm fine. It looks like your kidnapper let you know his identity so he could lead us straight into a deadly trap."

"Wyatt—" Zane froze for a millisecond before running for the house.

She climbed to her feet and dashed after Zane. Had she found Wyatt's hiding place in the cellar? And if so, how scared the boy must be being locked in the dark!

THREE

Zane raced through the open door with Bliss right behind him. He hurried down the steps of what appeared to be an old storm cellar with access in the closet. Moist, dank air met him. Concrete walls surrounded him, but no child.

Bliss picked up an open box of animal crackers and examined the contents. "He's been here."

Zane's jaw twitched. "That could've been down here for a long time."

She shook her head, removed a cracker and snapped it in half. "These aren't stale."

His grandson had been here. He glanced around, his gaze landing on a shelf above Bliss's head. "There's a doll."

She smiled. "Most boys would call that an action figure."

He shrugged and didn't touch the toy cowboy in case there were fingerprints on it. "We'll let the investigators see if they can find anything else."

"Lawrence brought your grandson back here." Bliss glanced at him. "They can't be far away. Maybe even on this property."

"I was thinking the same thing."

Her gaze fixed on the toy. "Chandler may be able to use the action figure to get Wyatt's scent."

That was good news. Chandler and his K-9 should be here shortly. Zane followed her up the steps and into the living room. While she made a call, he stepped outside and looked over the horizon as the dark clouds forbade the morning sun to shine. It was impossible to see how far this place went back for all the trees.

Would Lawrence be foolish enough to hide his grandson here?

But the biggest question was if Lawrence wanted the Texas Rangers to find who planted evidence against his brother, *if* someone planted evidence, then why secure a grenade to take them out?

Or was all this just a ploy to get investigators here to sabotage them?

His cell phone rang. "Adcock."

"Lieutenant, this is Chasity. I located your daughter. She's en route to Liberty as we speak."

Why hadn't Sage called him herself? His number hadn't changed. They hadn't spoken in years, but to not talk to him in a time of an emergency was beyond bitter. Had he been such a bad dad? Success in his career had been easy, but not so in his relationships. They had to put the past behind them, if for no other reason than for the boy's sake. "Did you learn any information from her?"

"No, sir, I'm sorry to say, except that she'd been in the hospital. Understandably, she's quite upset. Pascal police sent me the report. It stated Sage was pushing a cart with the boy walking beside her. When the perpetrator pulled up in an older-model black Chevy truck, he grabbed her son and threw him into his vehicle.

Before he could shut the door, your daughter got her hands in the door, trying to get him back. She chased after them but fell and was dragged over thirty feet before losing her grip.

"Jason Cunningham, the chief of police in Liberty, is setting up a command post, and Sage will be there. Her estimated time of arrival is ninety minutes."

"Thanks." He clicked off. He tried not to think about how close his daughter had come to being seriously injured. Maybe they would find Wyatt by the time his mother got here. He prayed it would be so.

Bliss walked out and made a beeline to him. "Something's bothering me."

"What's that?"

"You said Lawrence Weaver wanted us to find evidence. Why try to kill us?"

"I know. That question keeps crossing my mind, too. Maybe it's a setup and is a case of revenge. Could be the older brother wants us to suffer, like he'll mourn the loss of his brother after the execution." And if that were true, Lawrence had no intention of keeping Wyatt alive. The thought was too painful to consider, but Zane couldn't make the idea go away. He'd worked too many cases in which the suspect had no qualms about killing.

She nodded. "Or he'd rather us work to find evidence and not spend time searching for your grandson."

"Maybe. But then why take someone important to me? Taking my family would guarantee we couldn't be scared away. We wouldn't with anyone, but Lawrence wouldn't know that." He went on to relay what he'd learned from Chasity's call.

Bliss frowned. "I'm thankful Sage wasn't seriously hurt."

Zane's phone dinged as a new text message came through. He glanced down. The message from Chasity said Weaver didn't own other properties, but there was a vacation rental he used twice a year. She attached the link to the property. He clicked on the site and scrolled through the twelve pics. It looked to be a houseboat named *Sweet Betty Lou* on a small island in Lake Texoma.

He glanced up at Bliss's questioning gaze. "I need to go. I've got a location that needs checking out."

"I'm going with you."

"You don't want to wait for your team?"

"I've already let Chandler know where I found the action figure. I'm hoping the toy will carry the victim's scent. But, no, to answer your question. I want to keep looking. Between the K-9 team and your man with the drone, they can do more here than me."

He hated the term *victim* when referring to his grandson. It sounded impersonal, but he knew it was just semantics. "Let's go, then."

They hurried to get in his truck. He put in a call to Ranger Dryden, filled him in on the grenade and warned him to watch out for more traps. "Chasity sent me the address to a houseboat on a small island in Lake Texoma, where our man has stayed numerous times. The place shows to be rented, and she's trying to get a hold of the owners. Could you secure me a boat at one of those rental places?"

"Yes, sir. We'll be at Weaver's place in thirty-eight minutes. I talked with Ranger O'Neill a little bit ago. He confirmed with the Pascal Police Department that Wyatt was taken in Pascal, Texas, from a grocery store parking lot. He's talking with the chief right now to get the details."

"Good. Chasity received the kidnapping report earlier, and hopefully the chief can add more details. Bliss Walker and I are on the way to check out the houseboat. Her K-9 team with the Bring the Children Home Project are on their way to search the woods. Keep me updated."

After he disconnected, Bliss asked thoughtfully, "You think it's more likely Lawrence is hiding Wyatt in the houseboat instead of the woods here?"

"I'm not certain of anything, but it seems more probable. If Lawrence is here, he could easily slip past the two of us." As Zane was pulling out, he glanced over his shoulder toward the woods. It was possible that Lawrence was watching them to see if they'd been injured. Seeing no one, Zane turned onto the rock road in the direction of the highway.

They'd gone about a quarter of a mile when something glistened from the trees, and Zane jerked on the wheel just as several rounds from a high-powered rifle rent the air. "Take cover."

He hit the accelerator, bounced across the shallow ditch, and then slammed on the brakes behind the trunk of a huge pecan tree.

Bliss was on the side of the shooter, but she already had her gun ready and the window down.

Zane got out, keeping his head low, and moved behind the bed of his truck. Distant lightning gave just enough light to see someone running through the woods. The man shot again.

Squeezing the trigger of his gun, Zane returned fire. Bliss shot two rounds.

And then all was silent.

She asked quietly, "Do you see the gunman?"

"No." He continued to look for movement but saw nothing. "I'm going to check if the man's been hit."

"I've got your back."

"Stay here."

He crossed the ditch and entered the thick woods. Poison ivy and thistles came from every direction. He stepped carefully, trying not to get the itchy stuff on him.

Movement came from behind him. "I asked you to stay there."

"You asked for my help, and I told you I'd be your backup."

She was used to being in charge, but so was he. Some things hadn't changed since they'd dated years ago, but they could discuss leadership roles later. The ground was slick and muddy, but it should silence their movements.

She whispered, "Three o'clock."

He squinted to the right. Something dark presented itself under a tree. Was that a person kneeling against the trunk?

Bliss moved closer to him. "I'll cover you if you want to go in."

"Don't shoot me even by accident." He didn't look at her but could guess her reaction.

Staying low, he moved to the next tree, and then another. A large, murky puddle blocked his path. He skirted it and stopped beside an oak. He still wasn't certain if the shadow was a man. Sometimes things in the woods looked like an animal or person but were the shadows of overgrown vegetation or a fallen log.

He aimed his gun. "This is Lieutenant Texas Ranger Zane Adcock. Drop your weapon." When the figure didn't move, he repeated the command.

Nothing. Was the man conscious? A glance at the ground didn't show signs of blood or footprints. He stepped closer, ready for the unexpected. A low limb hung in his way, and he ducked to go under it.

A gunshot broke the silence.

A bullet whizzed past his ear. Zane dropped to the ground and turned, looking for the source.

Behind him, another gun went off. Bliss!

A tall man took off at a sprint from over thirty feet away in the opposite direction.

Zane glanced over his shoulder to make sure Bliss hadn't moved into his line of fire, but he heard a gasp and then a splash. She slid to her knee in the hole.

With his gun ready, he took off in the man's direction. He wove in and out of the woods, vines tugging at his jeans, and several times, his boots slipped in the muck. A deep ravine appeared in front of him. He slid down the bank, dragging his hand behind him to keep his balance. He hit the flowing water with a splash.

The water came up to his knees and flowed swiftly. A glance up the other side presented no easy way up. Right or left? Right went toward the road and left deeper into the woods. He chose left.

He kept an eye out for signs left by the man but saw nothing. After several minutes, an engine sounded in the distance and faded away.

Zane had gone the wrong way. Frustrated, he trudged out of the ravine and headed back toward Bliss. A couple of minutes later, they met on the trail. "Let's go."

"I heard a vehicle drive away."

"Me too." He nodded. When they got back in the cab, he turned his truck around and drove slowly up the road, searching for the other vehicle, but saw nothing. He called Ranger Dryden to give him an update so he would know to be on the lookout for the gunman.

He turned onto the main highway.

"I don't like this." Bliss looked in her mirror. "Do you think the shooter was Lawrence?"

"I don't know. If so, then the man doesn't believe his brother was set up. He just wants to take my grandson and then kill me."

"Maybe. But why you? And the grenade would've blown up anyone who entered the underground room. Maybe he wants to take out any law enforcement."

"Could be. But Lawrence doesn't have a criminal record. Not even a speeding ticket. His wife didn't have a record and was a schoolteacher for over twenty years. Why become violent now?"

"Doesn't make sense." Bliss's words melted away as she stared out the window. He thought she was done when she whispered, "I'm sorry about misidentifying the shadows. I thought it was a person."

"Could happen to anyone. It did look like the silhouette of a man hunched against the tree, and if you had not warned me, I might have run up on the shooter."

Bliss's brown eyes met his. He thought she was going to say something, but she turned back to the window, her face a still, lifeless expression. A grim twist tugged at her mouth.

What was the somberness all about? Back when they'd dated, she'd been a constant source of optimism, a gusto for life. It was one of the things that had attracted him—she'd been supportive of his career choice and loved that he lived on a ranch. Preferred the country life. She was eager to start her own career but had gladly accepted his marriage proposal and preferred a short engagement.

It wasn't just with him, either. Her enthusiasm was contagious, which made her a great leader.

Another look in her direction showed a stiff posture and had him wanting to comfort her. But he couldn't do that. She was here to help find his grandson. Nothing more.

He needed to learn more about her son. It was obvious that her son not being found until after years of searching had taken its toll. Everyone who had been in law enforcement more than a few years had that one case they could never forget—something that rocked their being and had them asking if the career was worth it. No doubt her son's case fit that situation.

He felt that same way about Sage and Wyatt. Had his career cost him his family? When was enough enough? He honestly didn't know. Zane ate, slept and bled the Texas Rangers.

As they traveled down the highway to the lake, Bliss finally turned toward him. "Tell me about how Weaver was arrested and wound up on death row."

Talking about the case was better than watching her worry. "I'd worked several homicides while with the Texas State Troopers, but this was my first homicide as a Texas Ranger, and I remember it had been an airtight case. Marvin Larson, a Liberty police officer, had been killed when he went to serve a warrant at the home of Sean Weaver, who was suspected of dealing drugs. Not only was Larson, a nineteen-year veteran with the department, dead, but Sean was found with a bullet wound to the chest, a pistol lay beside his hand, and several bags of cocaine were on the floor. By the position of the bodies, it appeared Officer Larson surprised Weaver, and Weaver shot at the officer but missed. Larson then shot Sean, but not before the suspect got off another round. Sean was injured and rushed to the hospital, where he survived.

"Once Sean recovered, he claimed he had no memory of the shooting, just that he had come home from work from his factory job. He admitted he had occasionally used cocaine in the past but denied he was still using or that he had ever sold it."

Her brow wrinkled. "And now Lawrence claims evidence had been planted against his brother."

"Yeah. And more than likely, Lawrence simply can't buy that his family member was capable of murder. Not that unusual."

She sighed. "I agree."

"I don't appreciate the game of cat and mouse. And using my grandson as leverage forces law enforcement to divide our time between looking into the sixteen-year-old murder case and trying to find Wyatt. Lawrence has nothing to lose."

Several minutes later, Zane turned down the highway near the Denison Dam. He checked his rearview mirror again, but still there was no sign of anyone following them, like he'd half expected. It'd been a wet year, and with all the rain over the past couple of weeks, the spillway had almost crested—something that had only happened twice in the dam's history.

Even with the floodgates open, the massive man-made lake swelled to its banks, threatening to overflow. He hoped the conditions didn't stop them from accessing the island and houseboat.

Morning traffic was almost zilch since it was summer and school was out. Last night's storms would also delay many would-be travelers.

Bliss said, "I hate to see the water up so high. If the water goes over the spillway, it will destroy the banks of the Red River on both the Texas and Oklahoma sides. That's a lot of homes and cropland. Hopefully, we won't get more rain."

"I agree, but rain is in the forecast. And according to those clouds, it's about to open up."

Bliss leaned forward and looked up at the sky. "I'm praying Wyatt is in the houseboat and we can get to him before the storm hits."

"I was thinking the same thing." A few minutes later, he pulled up to the dock as raindrops hit the windshield. No other people or fishermen were about.

A huge streak of lightning split the sky.

"Do you think we should wait?" Her hand was on the door handle like she was debating staying in the vehicle. "Being on the water during an electrical storm isn't smart. I just checked the radar on my weather app. Looks like a big system."

Zane eyed her. "I'd like for you to stay here, Bliss. It's too dangerous. But it's possible there's a scared little boy on a houseboat in a storm, and I'm going in after him. Maybe I can get there before the worst of it hits. I wish we could be helicoptered in, but we'd have to wait for the storm to pass for that, too."

She shook her head. "I'm going with you."

I won't need you. The words hung on the tip of his tongue, but one look at the determination in her strong posture and set jaw, and he knew there was little chance of changing her mind. He'd seen that stance before. As much as it pained him to admit, he needed her.

Bliss wanted to wait for the storm to subside, but mostly, she didn't want to take a chance on making another mistake.

And now probably wasn't the best time to remind Zane she wasn't a good swimmer. She could kick around in a pool, but never had been able to swim far. With doubts plaguing her, something in her consciousness wouldn't let her turn her back on this man. "Let's go."

"All right. But there's no guarantee the boy is even here, especially if Lawrence was the one shooting at us. But I pray my grandson is on that boat. The longer we sit here, the longer we give Lawrence time to come back."

If the boy was still alive. The thought came unbidden, but she didn't say it. "I still want to go."

He reached into the back seat and grabbed a raincoat and his duster. He handed the raincoat to her, and he shoved his plastic-covered Stetson on his head.

Emotion danced in the lieutenant's eyes, and she wondered what he was thinking. The conditions were treacherous for a rescue, but rarely were circumstances perfect when running into the unknown.

Bliss said a quick prayer, asking God to watch over them, before she opened her door and jogged to the dock and under the awning. Her gut swirled at the prospect of finding little Wyatt—a strange mixture of uncertainty and hope. Maybe the search would be over in the next hour. She prayed for Zane's sake that they would find his grandson unharmed.

A man with white hair hunched on a barstool behind the counter and eyed them as they walked through the open door. He wore a pair of striped overalls and a fishing hat. "You need to give the storm time to let up before going on the water."

"My officer called ahead to reserve a craft."

"He did. But being out there—" he pointed "—in the weather is asking for trouble."

Zane replied quickly. "That's my decision. Too many things at work here."

"Suit yourself," the older man mumbled. "It's not like I can't use the business. It's in bay nine. I'll need you to sign the waiver." He shoved the paper across the counter, and Zane scribbled on the form.

The lieutenant took the keys from the older man and hurried out the door with her keeping stride with him.

As soon as Bliss stepped into the open, rain pelted her waterproof hood, and the wind slammed into her back. The ski boat had a small awning to cover the driver. She hurried under it and took the seat opposite Zane.

He fired up the engine and backed out of the bay. Even though the posted speed limit was five miles per hour, with no other boats around, he opened the throttle. They shot across the rolling waves toward the west. The rumbling thunder could barely be heard over the wind and the engine.

She gripped the sides of the boat and kept her head down as the pelting rain felt like tiny needles. The boat flew over the waters, going airborne, and each hit pounded her body.

He checked his cell phone, she assumed for the location of the island.

"How far is it?"

He returned his attention to the lake. "About twelve minutes."

That was an excruciatingly long time in these conditions. The darks clouds swirled. A streak of lightning lit up the sky, followed by a loud boom. Her heart raced. That was much too close.

Normally, she was laser-focused on a case and didn't allow herself to become too anxious calculating the dangers. But this was different. Going against Mother Nature could be far more dangerous, and the waves were so boisterous. She sat in her seat and couldn't help but notice the hazards. Squeezing her eyes shut, she prayed again for their safety.

Seconds ticked by, and then minutes. The movement made her head swim and her stomach roil.

"Are you okay?" he shouted over the noise.

She opened her eyes to see Zane looking at her. "I'm fine," she yelled. "The bouncing on the waves is making me dizzy."

"Almost there."

She drew a deep breath. The storm worsened. The skies had grown darker and the winds gustier.

An island appeared in the distance. Trees bent in the wind, and waves crashed against the shore. They drew closer. An older two-deck houseboat tossed in the water. Thankfully, it was still tied to the wooden dock, but by the way it swayed, only one rope must still be attached. How much longer could the craft hold on before it ripped a hole in the side or was dragged into open waters?

Zane aimed their ski boat directly at the dock, making her cringe. At the last minute, he jerked his wheel to the side and drove the boat onto the shore. His jaw twitched—a sign he was determined—and she knew he must be eager to see if his grandson was on that boat. He hurried to the bow and jumped onto the beach.

She scrambled from her seat and slid across after him. The houseboat bounced high in the water and crashed back down. The faded letters spelled out *Sweet Betty Lou* on the side. *Please, Lord, be with Zane so that he doesn't hurt himself getting on that boat.*

Her heart raced, and she shoved her dripping hair out of her face.

He jogged across the pier and had just about reached the boat when a child's voice carried on the wind. She whipped around, her gaze going inland to the trees. A splash of color mixed with green undergrowth and a figure carrying a child disappeared into the foliage.

She turned back. "Wait. Zane!"

Boom! Lightning struck the upper deck, and the flash was so intense it temporarily blinded her.

She blinked away the brightness as flames fell onto the pier.

Her heart stuttered as she witnessed Zane scramble to his feet just as fire kicked up behind him, blocking his path to land—the boat blazed in front of him. She moved closer and yelled, "Wyatt's not on the boat. Come back!"

Deafening thunder shook the ground, and boisterous waves crashed over her boots, drowning out her warning as Zane continued for the houseboat.

An image of Mitchell's face flitted through her mind. Just like all the Bring the Children Home cases, her mission was clear—save the child. No matter her recent mistakes, indecision had never been a problem.

She turned and bolted in the direction the man had taken the four-year-old. *Please, Lord, help me reach the child in time. And protect the ranger.*

FOUR

Bliss raised her arm to block the rain, but the effort had little effect as a wind gust blew the moisture into solid sheets. She headed inland, away from Zane and toward where the child had been taken. Water ran on the beach in fast-flowing streams.

Drooping vines hung in her path, slapping her as she ran by. She carried her gun in her hand but was careful not to drop it due to it being slippery. A quick glance ahead showed an open sandy area with a sagging volleyball net, but no sign of the kidnapper.

Since she was in an unobstructed clearing, she paused to take a good look around to make certain she hadn't run into a trap. Lightning struck close, followed by deafening thunder. Her body shook, but she didn't see anyone. Being in the open was not safe, and she felt the need to keep moving. Her boots squished through the puddle-ridden beach toward a small grove of trees.

An engine barely rose above the pounding of the rain. She glanced back to where Zane had abandoned their boat, but it didn't sound like it was coming from that direction. It was to her left. She took off at a sprint.

The rumble grew louder. She panted for breath as she set her path straight for the engine.

Then she heard the cry of a child.

Adrenaline kept her moving, and she shoved the dangers to the back of her mind. As she pushed her way through the opening in the trees, a Jet Ski nabbed her attention. "Wait!"

A man held a boy in front of him and looked up at her. She couldn't be sure, but it sounded as if the watercraft died.

She sucked air as she rushed to the beach, holding the gun to her side while keeping a watch on the man to make certain he didn't shoot at her. The Jet Ski bobbed on the swells like a bucking bronco as the guy attempted to get it started again.

Save the boy. The thought repeated through her brain as she tried to move faster. Hopefully, Lawrence would not force her to use her weapon. Only ten yards away. She waved her hands. "Wait."

Through the wind and rain, their gazes connected. Desperation reverberated back at her. She made it to the water's edge, her boots sinking in the mud and creating a challenge. But she kept going, victory within reach. The waves hit her with incredible force, making it impossible to swim, so she continued fighting and moving forward.

The little boy looked at her, fear on his face. His lip puckered, and he cried.

"Stop crying, Wyatt," the man demanded.

The engine revved to life.

The man glanced over his shoulder, and she aimed her gun. "Stop, Lawrence. Don't harm the boy." The storm was so loud, she didn't know if he could hear her words.

She reached the craft, and a wave slammed her into

the side of the Jet Ski and caused her to go under. As terror threatened, the weapon slipped from her hand, and she tried to get her feet underneath her.

As she surfaced, she saw the end of a gun barrel staring her in the face.

She ducked under just as the machine sucked in water. The craft took off, but not before slamming into her back. She looked up in time to see the two escape. Lightning struck the lake less than a hundred yards away.

Pain radiated throughout her body. She prayed she hadn't made the wrong decision by forcing them into open waters. Her breath hitched as she watched them jump waves, the Jet Ski going airborne, and Wyatt slid from his seat.

The craft landed on its side and was swallowed by the swell.

She gasped. *Oh no!*

The Jet Ski surfaced upside down but neither passenger was in sight. Swallowing her fear, she swam into the perilous waters with one thing on her mind.

Save the boy.

Zane struggled for air as the intense heat beat down on him. The *Sweet Betty Lou* was totally engulfed. A check of the lower level had produced no child, but he couldn't leave without checking the upper deck.

As he climbed the ladder, the boat leaned precariously toward the water, and a gaping hole stood in front of him. He realized his mistake too late. His foot slid into the opening, and his boot wedged in between a metal railing and the broken slide. Flames bellowed and swelled with the wind gusts. The rain wasn't powerful enough to put out the fire. He twisted and yanked until his foot was free.

"Wyatt. Are you here?"

No answer. If Wyatt had been here, it was unlikely he could have survived the damage, but Zane hurried across to the other side, just to be sure. Smoke sifted through the pounding rain, and there was no sight of his grandson. Certain the boy wasn't there, he moved to go back to the ladder.

Crack!

The portion of the floor he was standing on swayed and then collapsed. He half fell, half slid down to the lower deck and hit his thigh on a protruding panel. He looked up just as several boards pummeled him. There was barely time to block the brunt of the impact with his arm.

A loud whooshing came from the flames as the boat slammed into the pier. The side facing the dock dipped into the water, causing his edge to ride up. The houseboat was going down.

Zane turned to jump just as an enormous swell hit, sending the floor straight up. He fell into the lake and attempted to swim away from the sinking boat, but the *Sweet Betty Lou* came down, knocking him deeper. His boots and jeans weighed him down even more.

As hard as he tried, the waves were too strong and pulled him farther into the lake. His mind whirled with doubt as fear settled in his chest. He had to use the force to drive him. Instead of fighting, he attempted to relax and ride the swell up to distance himself from the houseboat. Lightning flashed, and he managed to keep his head above the surface as he traveled farther away. Once he was thirty yards from the wreckage, he turned his efforts toward making it to the shore. He rode another surge that brought him near the beach. A couple more bellows, and his knees hit the ground. He crawled the rest of the way out.

As soon as he climbed to his feet, he looked around for Bliss. A glance at the dock showed only wooden poles sticking up, and the remaining section was in broken pieces and floating away. His rented boat was still on the beach, but Bliss was nowhere in sight. He cupped his hands. "Bliss!"

His heart drummed fast in his chest. Had she been on the pier when it fell into the water? Or had the shooter returned?

Drenched to the bone, he crossed the sand into the wooded area. He never should've allowed her to come with him. Even though she'd wanted to search for Wyatt, he remembered she wasn't a good swimmer. His gaze remained on the ground, praying he'd spot her footprints as he made his way to the trees.

Please, God, don't let her be in the water.

FIVE

The waves pounded her, making her gulp water and fight to breathe as she swam to the bobbing Jet Ski. For every two feet of progress, she was knocked back by another wave. Her arms stung, and her body was fraught with exhaustion.

A giant wave slammed into her and sucked her under. The out-of-control swirling motion made her lose her direction. Her lungs burned, and in a panic, she kicked her legs as hard as she could. She surfaced and gasped for oxygen just as another surge hit. This time, she managed to stay above.

In a controlled frenzy, she searched for signs of the child. Before she reached the craft, something red hovered underneath the surface. It could be the man, but she moved to meet it. As she neared, the sight of a small kicking figure caused her to hope.

Thank You, God. Please help me save him.

Her lungs burned, but adrenaline spurred her on. She fought to keep her head above water when another wave sent the body to her. The boy floated to the top. She lunged for him but was swept backward and out of reach. *No!*

Out of the corner of her eye, an arm splashed. The man swam toward her.

With pure determination, she tried again and snagged the boy by his shirt. She pulled him against her chest, making sure his head was above water. Was he alive?

Even though the man was coming for her, the boy's life took priority. She rolled onto her back with Wyatt in her arms, allowing the swells to push her. Emotion filled her. He was safe in her arms. "Wyatt." She stared into the blue face and turned him over, pressing his back into her chest. As they fought the storm, she fisted her hands, put them in the center of his breastbone and performed chest compressions. Water continued to swallow them, but she did the best she could.

Seconds later, they washed up onshore. As she struggled to her feet with him in her arms, the boy choked and coughed water. Finally, he vomited. Relief was short-lived, as they needed to get to the lieutenant. But a glance over her shoulder showed the kidnapper had almost made it to the beach.

They needed to hide. She sprinted for the cover of the trees, but a tall, grassy area at the shoreline caught her attention, and she bolted for it.

A wooden frame covered in camouflage netting emerged. It looked like an old collapsed duck blind. While still in motion, she slid under the covering. Straw-like grass poked at her, but she was able to get down in her casket-size box. The container sagged, not giving her much room. She lay on her side, propped on her elbow.

The boy's coloring had improved, but he continued to cough.

"Wyatt," she whispered, "I'm here to help you."

Confused and fearful brown eyes stared at her.

She pushed his wet hair back from his forehead as she looked him over. His breathing was steady but raspy. Even though Wyatt's features were darker, the child was close to the same size as Mitchell when her son disappeared. Fierce protectiveness consumed her as she held the boy in her arms. Oh, how she had wished for this moment with her own child.

The storm seemed to be growing weaker, and the rain had almost stopped.

Heavy panting sounded from outside.

She placed a finger to her lips. "Be very quiet."

He blinked. He was either too weak to respond or understood, for he became still.

A gust of wind hit the blind, causing the grass on the roof to blow. Instinctively, she rubbed her hand across the boy's arm, hoping to offer comfort. What must it be like to be stolen from your mother at a grocery store, be kept in a cellar and then brought on an island during a treacherous thunderstorm? The boy must be frightened beyond belief. Bliss's motherly impulses kicked in, making her want to get him to safety more than life itself.

Seconds ticked by, but no more sounds from the kidnapper.

She whispered, "My name is Bliss. I'm going to help you."

His lip turned down. "I want my mama."

Her chest constricted. *And his mama needs her child.* Her voice automatically lowered, and she nodded. "I'm going to take you to her. Okay? But we must be very quiet."

He frowned. "I want to go now."

"We have to wait for the bad guy to be caught."

"I don't like him," he shrilled. His arm trembled, and he repeated, "I want my mama."

Pulling him into a hug, she clung to him, hoping to soothe him. If the child became louder, the man might hear. "Wyatt, I'm going to help you. I'm working with the police."

"No." He pushed against her.

"Calm down. We don't want the bad man to hear us."

"No." He slapped at her. "Let me go. I want to go home."

Her heart raced. How to make him understand? "Wyatt, it's okay. I'm going to take you to your mama. We have to be patient."

Where was Zane? She hoped he got here soon.

She wanted to make a run for the boat, but what if Lawrence was still close by?

A man's voice called, "Wyatt. Where are you?"

The boy's head jerked in the direction of the sing-songy voice.

"It's okay." Every muscle in her body tensed. That was not Zane. Again, she put her finger to her lips and prayed the boy would remain silent. Carefully, she scooted to the opening of the crude duck blind. Sand clung to her skin, and she spun around on her bottom so that her feet were near the exit for a fast escape.

The wind blew through the contraption, blocking out many of the sounds. She watched the doorway. Were her footprints visible or had the rain washed them away?

Her gaze stayed latched on the opening.

Suddenly a man's face appeared in the gap.

Wyatt screamed, and Bliss kicked out with both

feet. Her boot connected with his nose, and he stumbled back.

She shoved herself to her knees, secured Wyatt in her grasp and ducked through the opening. She took off and tried to sidestep the man on the ground. She almost made it, but a hand grabbed her foot.

The boy continued to cry as she kicked, trying to free herself. Somehow she managed to stay on her feet.

"Let him go or I'll kill ya," the man shouted. A gun glistened in the man's shirt pocket.

If she could get her hands on the weapon…

The kidnapper's gaze connected with hers. He released her boot and grabbed for his gun.

With Wyatt still in her grasp, she bolted toward the trees through the wet sand.

A gunshot sounded.

She flinched at the noise but kept going. Wyatt was not going back into the kidnapper's hands.

"Bliss Walker, stop. I don't want to kill you. I just want to know who framed my brother!"

Good. Then don't shoot. She continued to sprint for cover when another blast went off. Pain exploded down her leg. Then she was falling.

As agony spread throughout her body, she clung to the child.

No matter the cost, she wouldn't allow the boy back into the arms of his abductor.

Please, Zane. Where are you?

Gunshots had Zane moving swiftly through the downed vegetation left by the storm. He'd circled over half the island searching for Bliss.

When he ran through the open brush, he spotted her

lying on the ground, blood soaking her pants. He rushed to her side. "Are you all right?"

She waved at him with her hand. "Go. Go find Wyatt. I had him in my arms." She moved her hands to her chest. "Lawrence shot me and took your grandson. His Jet Ski sank, and there's no way for him to escape except on our boat."

Zane's lungs tightened at the thought of leaving her here injured. Then a faraway cry reached his ears.

"Go! Get to the boat."

He bolted in the direction of the cry. But as he ran through the dense woods, two large trees lay broken on the trail. He skirted the fallen oaks to the right and off the path. Threading his way through the brush, he came out on the side and picked up his speed again. Zane worked out regularly, but it had been years since he'd been in a foot race, especially in boots. His breath came in sharp gasps as he made tracks across the island.

Surely, the suspect would have had a harder time since he was carrying Wyatt.

Please, Lord, help get my grandson before Lawrence disappears with him.

But as he neared the beach, the sound of a motor puttered in the distance. Struggling for breath, he advanced on the boat as it backed into the water. His gaze latched on to the squirming and kicking boy in the man's arms. As Zane's boots hit the water, their boat took off at a fast speed from the shore into the waters. Zane aimed his gun, but they were bouncing and moving too quickly to get a good shot at the driver.

He stopped and rested his hands on his knees as he tried to catch his breath. His stomach hardened as he watched the boat disappear on the horizon. As soon as his panting slowed, he turned to go back for Bliss, but she was standing at the edge of the trees, leaning against a trunk for support. He hurried her way.

"Sit down."

"Did they get away?" Worry lines creased her forehead, but she allowed him to assist her to the ground.

"Yeah, they took off before I could catch them. When did you realize my grandson wasn't on the houseboat?"

"When we were on the pier. I yelled at you, but you couldn't hear me. I decided to go after the boy on my own."

Frustration descended on him. "You should've alerted me first. We could've had this guy. You don't have to do everything alone." At the strange expression on her face—a mixture of anger and hurt—he tried to calm his racing heart and lower his voice. "Let me call this in and then we need to talk."

He glanced at his wet cell phone and was glad to see he had reception. When Ranger Dryden answered, he gave him an update, asked him to pick them up, and called the hospital to alert them they needed to be ready for a gunshot victim.

After he clicked off, he sat on his haunches beside her. "Let me see that wound."

"I'm fine." Her voice was clipped, and she moved away. "I've already looked at it and it went through."

"I want you to have a doctor look at it."

"I will." She released a heavy sigh and then looked directly at him. "Don't ever tell me I shouldn't have gone for the child first."

A retort died on his lips at her clenched jaw and shiny eyes. "I didn't mean it like that."

"I will *always* try to save the child." Her lips trembled. *"Always."*

"I understand." His breath left him at the pain in her eyes. "Tell me what happened."

"You don't understand." Her statement was quick and certain. Her chin dropped to her chest. "I had Wyatt in my arms. He kept asking for his mama, and I told him I'd bring him to her. But I couldn't hang on. I let him go. Don't you understand?"

Not really. This was one of those times he thought it best not to say anything.

"He loved cowboys. His favorite toy was a cowboy and his horse, and he played with them all the time. He'd crawl through the house on his hands and knees, pretending to be a horse, and rear up while neighing. The barn and fences. Toy cattle."

Confusion at her words caused him to hesitate. She wasn't talking about Wyatt anymore. He knelt beside her. "Bliss…"

She fell into his arms. "Mitchell was the coolest kid ever. His smile would light up the world. A people pleaser. For a boy, he was very loving and didn't mind hugs and kisses. His favorite color was red, and he loved ketchup with his chicken nuggets. The day before he was abducted, he picked flowers for me from our yard—the little purple weed ones. I was busy cooking supper and put them in a glass of water." Her voice broke. "I don't even remember if I told him thank you."

He held her as she was racked with the tears. If he could trade places with her right now and take on all of her pain and hurt, he would. Since he couldn't, he embraced her gently and didn't say a word. He'd never felt so helpless.

For several moments, he kept his arms around her, feeling her raw emotion and grief. What had he been thinking to tell her not to save the child first?

Bliss had always been a strong, independent person. A natural leader. It was one of the things that had attracted him to her, but also the thing that annoyed him. She didn't always have to be so tough. But seeing her vulnerable undid him.

She sniffed and sat up as she wiped her eyes. "I'm sorry." A laugh escaped her lips. "You must think I've lost it."

"You have nothing to apologize for. I'm the one who wasn't thinking."

She looked at him and shook both fists. "I had him in my arms, Zane. In my grasp. How could I have lost him again? What is wrong with me?"

"Nothing is wrong with you." Her utter frustration and doubt stabbed his heart. "Tell me what happened."

"I heard a child's voice and saw someone disappear into the trees. I tried to get your attention, but you couldn't hear me over the storm. I pursued them across the island, and by the time I caught up, Lawrence was on a Jet Ski. He flipped it in the waves, but I was able to pluck Wyatt out of the water. We hid in an old duck blind until Lawrence found us. He threatened to shoot me if I didn't hand him over. Instead, I ran while carrying Wyatt. Lawrence shot me."

She'd run even after the kidnapper threatened to shoot her? "You're the gutsiest person I know. You did all you could." At her audible sigh, he continued. "I'm sorry for taking my frustrations out on you."

"I'll live."

He rubbed the back of his neck. Memories of their

past relationship surfaced, reminding him of how they used to argue. She'd left because she had a job offer, but things had been far from perfect. Right now, they needed to find Wyatt.

"I did what I thought was best." She gazed heavenward with her eyes squeezed shut. "But it's never enough."

His heart tightened. He'd felt that way many times, but this was different.

"One more thing. Lawrence again insisted we find evidence to clear his brother. He also begged me to stop running because he didn't want to shoot me. I think he was telling the truth. Which means there's someone else out there that wants us off this case."

"Like whoever killed Officer Larson."

"Exactly."

If Bliss was correct, then not only did they need to get his grandson back and find evidence to save Sean from execution, but they also had to dodge a cop killer's attacks. As he walked to the edge of the beach, he turned to see Bliss limping.

"Let me help."

She paused with her jaw clenched tightly. "I've got it."

"Then make me feel better." He scooped her up into his arms and carried her across the sand.

"Put me down."

He glanced at her. "Are you serious?"

She rolled her eyes. "No. I could use the help, but I feel ridiculous."

He noted her body was stiff, as if cringing against the pain. When they neared the water's edge, he put her gently on the ground. "Dryden should be here soon."

She leaned back with one hand in the sand and her leg stretched out.

"We need to talk."

Her mouth twisted into a frown. "About what?"

"Next time."

She looked at him with one eyebrow raised.

He held a finger in the air, letting her know to wait before she argued. "Next time let me know what's going on. You are the best in the business, which is why I asked for your help. But if I'd known Wyatt wasn't on the houseboat, I could've helped, and Lawrence never would have got away with the boy."

"I had to make a split-second decision. In my business, the whole mission is to save the child. I yelled to get your attention, but you couldn't hear me. I didn't want Wyatt to get away."

He stared at her, and she stared right back, facing off against each other. The moment stretched until it was no longer comfortable. "I wish you trusted me more."

"I do believe in your abilities, Zane. But I will always do what I think is best. Don't ask me to compromise my belief." The firm set of her jaw said she would not back down.

"I do, too. Which is why, with your injury, you should investigate from the office. If you're right, and Lawrence isn't the one who's attacked us, then find out who did."

Her icy expression went straight through him. As much as he wanted her with him, maybe he'd made a mistake. Not only was Bliss shot, but he seemed to anger everyone who worked with him. Sage blamed him. Bliss was angry.

But if it meant saving their lives, he'd do what he needed to.

SIX

Bliss lay on the hospital bed staring up at the ceiling. The pain from the gunshot wound had lessened to a dull throb. The doctor administered a local anesthesia before cleaning and stitching up the damage. A large bandage secured with sticky tape now covered her thigh. A lady had already given her dismissal instructions to rest for the next forty-eight hours, not to get the area wet and to see her primary physician in a week.

Fat chance of resting.

Bliss caught a glance of the mirror and ran her fingers through her hair, trying to fluff it. A drowned rat had more appeal. Going all night with no sleep didn't help. Not that she believed this was the time to worry about her appearance. Zane had more important things to think about, and she realized after losing her husband and son, she could never give her heart away again.

As she waited for the nurse to return with her prescription, she wondered if Zane regretted asking her to help find his grandson. In all the missing children cases her team had worked, never had the child been in her arms only for her to lose him again. Her throat tightened as frustration ate away at her. She couldn't get distracted.

Doubt plagued her. What would she do if Wyatt wasn't found again? The thought was almost unbearable. How could she survive knowing he'd been in her grasp?

She had prayed to God for help to save the children, but she'd failed. Did she need to walk away from Zane and let someone else step in?

Zane claimed she should've waited on him instead of chasing after Wyatt. No way. That was how she'd lost Mitchell's trail. A witness had described a black Suburban that left the scene of the accident. She'd been prepared to check out the lead immediately, but her boss, Daniel Bryant, who didn't even want her on the case, had finally reneged and let her ride along with another marshal. By the time they caught up to the SUV, the vehicle had been abandoned in the parking lot of a mall—later to be determined it had been stolen hours earlier. The kidnapper had gotten away without a trace. Even though the marshals thought it was a case of being in the wrong place at the right time, Bliss believed the kidnapper had targeted Mitchell. The problem was their delayed response because the marshals were more concerned with protocol than moving quickly.

A mistake she vowed never to repeat.

Bliss had lost her chance of a family with Adam's death. Zane didn't need to lose his, too. After having Mitchell, her life became more complicated working with the marshals. Her son had been a welcome surprise, but still her life had become more challenging while juggling a baby, work and a husband. When her son was three, Adam voiced his desire for another child. But she was the one who wanted to wait. Finally, when Adam turned four, she agreed to try. She got pregnant almost instantly but miscarried two months later. The loss hit her hard, and she needed time to grieve before trying one more time.

Her doctor had said there was no medical reason she couldn't have another child and she could expect a trouble-free pregnancy. This was her second miscarriage, but she'd told no one about the first loss.

She didn't learn of that pregnancy until after she'd broken her engagement to Zane, and by then, she was in Atlanta.

A week before Adam died, she finally agreed to try again.

It was too late. She lost her husband, son and hope of another child. Several friends suggested she remarry after a year, but she couldn't do it. She wanted to find Mitchell first. Being independent wasn't a bad thing, but sometimes she wished for a busy and boisterous house. Even grandkids were out of the question now.

"Here's your medication for antibiotics and pain." The woman whisked into the room and handed her a sheet of paper, went over the instructions that were printed on it and asked if she had any questions. When Bliss shook her head, the nurse said, "You're free to go."

Bliss shrugged into a sitting position and stood. The discomfort was barely noticeable, but she'd been injured too many times not to know that as soon as the anesthesia wore off, the pain would be back.

When she walked out of the room, Zane was casually leaning against the wall. His gaze met hers, assessing her.

She'd never cared to be pampered, and she waved a hand at him. "I'm fine."

"Sure you are. You haven't changed none, have you?"

"Not one bit." He knew she hated showing weakness. As she stepped past him, she tried to hide her smile and walked with only a minor limp.

He chuckled and followed her out of the hospital. When they got in his truck, he said, "I'm taking you home."

"No, you're not. I'm still on the case."

"That's not smart."

He didn't understand. She had to find Wyatt. Not only to help reunite the boy with his family but also for her own sake. No matter the cost, she had to keep searching. If she didn't, it would be the death of who she was as a person. She turned to him. "I don't have a boss anymore, Zane. I *am* the boss, and I say I don't need to go to my place. When Wyatt's home with his mama, I'll go home."

"Even though I disagree, I appreciate it, Bliss." His voice came out low and raspy.

She'd promised Wyatt to take him to his mama. She intended to keep her word.

Frustration bit at Zane as they pulled out of the hospital. They had been so close but had failed. Not only was a child's life at stake, but his whole family's was— what was left of it.

Almost as if she could read his thoughts, she turned to him. "How is your family?" At his raised eyebrows in question, she was quick to clarify. "I meant your parents and Cliff. It's been years..."

"Mom and Dad are fine. They are enjoying retirement, and except for Dad having a knee replacement last year, both are in good health. Did you know they sold all their livestock and farm equipment only to buy it back?"

"What?" She laughed. "No, I hadn't heard."

Zane smiled. "Mom had been after him to slow down. Dad finally auctioned everything, and they took a three-month vacation, traveling to all the places Mom had always wanted to visit. She even talked him into taking her on a Caribbean cruise."

A smile lit Bliss's face. "I can't imagine your dad on a ship. Please tell me your mom bought him a Hawaiian shirt and a pair of shorts."

"You know my parents well. She did, but he refused to wear them. He wore his jeans and boots."

She grinned. "That's funny. And you said he purchased the cattle back."

"Yeah. Dad's not happy unless he's working. He only bought back half the herd he used to run, but it keeps him busy." Growing up, Zane had been close to his immediate and extended family. His dad ranched while his mom stayed at home and occasionally taught as a substitute teacher at their elementary school.

"I was sorry to hear about your granddad. I know you were close."

"Thanks. He was a good man." Zane's love for law enforcement had come from his granddad, who'd been a sheriff of a small town. Back when he was a kid, Grandpa would tell old lawman stories while sitting around the supper table. Zane's favorite tale was Grandpa learning of a fugitive who had been at Miss Mattie's Bed and Breakfast for three weeks. After a shoot-out with the killer and Grandpa taking a bullet in the shoulder, he turned him over to the FBI. Much to his grandma's chagrin, Zane asked to hear it often. Probably everyone in the family realized his dreams even before he joined the Texas State Troopers to prepare for becoming a Texas Ranger.

"I always thought a lot of your parents. They were good to me. Is Cliff still married to Elizabeth?"

Cliff was Zane's younger brother. Bliss had had many a Sunday lunch at his folks' house. She never minded hanging out with his family, which was great, considering how close he was to them. "Yeah. Did you know they moved to Florida?"

"Really?" Her eyebrows rose.

He stared at her. "Why so surprised?"

"I guess I figured everyone in your family would stay in Texas. Seem to have strong roots here. Deep-in-the-heart-of-Texas type of thing."

He gave her a second look. Was she tossing that at him because he hadn't wanted to move to Atlanta to be with her? "Cliff is still playing stockbroker, and now that all three of their kids are in school, Liz is practicing law again."

"I'm happy for them." She turned back to the window.

All this talk about family made him think about his choices. With Bliss, when she walked out on him because he didn't want a long-distance relationship. And then losing his wife and then the fallout with his daughter. Was it simply his career choice or something that had to do with him personally?

"What did I miss while I was in the hospital?"

He was glad to turn his attention back to the case. "Not much. I called and checked on Sugar."

"Sugar?" Her eyebrow shot up.

"My seven-year-old Maltese."

"You have a toy breed?" She laughed. "I would've figured you for a Great Dane or a boxer."

He shook his head. "She was Sage's dog. We bought her as a puppy."

"Oh, I'm sorry." Bliss sobered.

"No problem. It's common to receive comments when people see the furball riding in my truck with me. She's spoiled rotten. Faye, my housekeeper, adores her and is good about helping out when I have a case that takes me away."

"It's great you have someone in your life to step in and help. I haven't had a pet in years because of my topsy-turvy life."

Zane didn't mention how Faye would video-chat so he could talk to the dog. "I'm blessed to have a lady to keep my home life going smooth. Besides checking on Sugar, I stopped by the police department, but the chief of police, Jason Cunningham, is moving the meeting place to the Liberty Community Center to give us more room since the Liberty PD station is small. I made a few calls to my Rangers. Luke Dryden is at Lawrence's house and has the drone in the air now that the storm has passed. I called off the search since we know Wyatt is not in the woods, but Dryden insisted on checking the property to see if there's any other structures that would make a good hiding place while he was there. Lawrence and Wyatt are on the move again. Several officers and three of the Bring the Children Home Project members are at the lake, searching for the boat and talking with people to see if anyone has seen the two. One man who was examining storm damage to his camper thought he saw a man and boy, but he was preoccupied and wasn't certain."

"I already said it, but I don't think Lawrence was the one shooting at us from the woods when we left his place."

"Maybe. But he could've hired someone. I'm not ruling anything out."

"For argument's sake, let's say it wasn't him. Wouldn't it make sense whoever framed Sean Weaver is the one targeting us?"

How could she so easily be convinced after meeting Lawrence? Bliss wasn't a person to be taken in and had always been a competent officer. Everyone in the field respected her work. He pulled into the parking lot of the Liberty Community Center. "Okay, for argument's sake, let's say Lawrence is telling the truth and his brother was set up. Are you saying it was someone in Liberty PD? Or a Texas Ranger?"

"Possibly." She nodded. "But it doesn't have to be. If drugs were involved, it could've been a dealer or someone else staying at the house. Or anyone that had reason to kill Officer Larson and frame Sean. Even a stranger. We need to find out who had reason to shoot Larson."

"There's not much time."

"I know." Brown knowing eyes flashed at him.

They got out and walked into the conference room. A news crew and several officers milled around, most of whom Zane didn't recognize.

Chandler Murphy, a K-9 handler on Bliss's team, strode over. "I heard about the shooting. Are you okay?"

"I'm fine." Bliss moved closer. "Have you learned anything more from the search?"

"No. The tracks ended at the road where the boat

was located. I'm sure the storm washed much of the evidence away."

"Hey, boss." Josie Hunt joined them but kept her voice low. "I found something interesting."

"Do we need to step outside?" Zane asked.

The investigator shook her head. "Good and bad news. Eight years ago, a dispatcher with the local sheriff's department, a man by the name of Ike Harris, got caught planting evidence against his ex-wife's new boyfriend. A neighbor's security camera filmed him in the boyfriend's car. He only received probation since it was his first offense. The deal is, authorities from a neighboring county believed he planted drugs in another case but were never able to prove it."

"So, what's the bad news?" Bliss asked.

"He died three years ago from a heart attack."

Bliss turned to Zane. "This may take more time with… What was his name? Harris. With Harris deceased. Do you think a judge will extend Sean Weaver's execution for a few more days?"

"I can try, but he sounded adamant when I talked to him earlier."

She nodded. "Can one of your men work with Josie on this? We'll need to interview friends and family, pronto."

"Exactly what I was thinking. I'll get Chasity Spears, our investigator." That was one thing about working with Bliss—they tended to think alike. He and Vivian had had a solid marriage, but they never quite connected like him and Bliss. Of course, they didn't argue like him and Bliss, either.

Josie said, "I know Chasity. I'll contact her, and we'll create a list."

"Good."

Zane moved a little closer so he could hear without talking loudly. A slight scent of her coconut shampoo drifted to him. It brought back memories of a happier time when they were dating and planning their life together. Both would work in law enforcement, and they had picked out land on the outside of town to build a house and a small ranch with horses. Except for the occasional butting of heads, life was exciting and promising. Then she'd received the opportunity to train for the US Marshals, and everything changed. Even though they had spirited disagreements, they had worked through their problems. But she was just as stubborn as he was and refused to bend or compromise on the job offer. Their quick breakup was messy, with each saying hurtful things. Both of them went their own ways and found new relationships. Later, both lost their families.

It was something he wished they didn't have in common.

He glanced at her and took in the stiff posture and clenched jaw. "You look like you're in a lot of pain. Why don't you go back to your office and assist in Sean Weaver's case while me and my guys search for my grandson?"

"I'm going to search for Wyatt. It's what I do." Her stern words told him she wouldn't change her mind. She held both palms up, and a pinched expression stared back at him. "I had him in my hands. He's such a sweet child, and he doesn't know what happened to his world."

When Zane had first asked her to help, Bliss had said she would work the case from her office. She struggled with dealing with the guilt of losing her son and now

Wyatt. He didn't want to add undue anxiety, but he refrained from saying the words aloud that he was concerned. The Bliss he knew didn't appreciate sympathy. He drew a deep breath and took her hand in his as he stared directly at her. He had to try.

"You're injured, and it won't help if you get hurt again. You may even slow us down. We have plenty of people looking for the boy."

"How many people are searching?"

The familiar female voice had Zane jerking his head toward the source. His daughter stood behind him with her arms crossed and her chin tilted upward. Her belly was swollen with child—maybe six months along or more. He released Bliss's hand. "Sage. I'm so glad you're here."

Hard green eyes bored into him. "Tell me why someone kidnapped my son from me at the grocery store."

You always choose your job over family. It was an accusation Vivian had made in one of their rare arguments just as fourteen-year-old Sage had walked into the room. Several times his daughter had tossed the comment in his face during the months prior to her turning eighteen, when she left for good. It wasn't true. Yes, he loved being a law officer, and sometimes the job required overtime, but family was important.

Vivian had taken the insult back as soon as the words were out, but Sage had clung to them. Zane knew his daughter must be scared to death, especially seeing she was pregnant, but she also would look for someone to take her anger out on. He weighed his comments carefully. Truth with a dose of consideration.

"A suspect abducted Wyatt to use as leverage against me to force me to look into an old case. The Texas

Rangers, Bring the Children Home Project—" he nodded toward Bliss "—and the Liberty Police Department are working around the clock to find your son."

Sage's attention channeled to Bliss as she scrutinized her. "You said you had Wyatt in your hands?"

"Yes. We—your dad and I—followed them to a houseboat rental on the lake. I was able to get your son away from the suspect for a few minutes but wasn't able to keep him."

He knew Bliss was keeping the details of the shooting away from Sage so as not to cause more alarm.

"You let him go?" His daughter's lips curled. "How could you?"

"Sage, please." He stepped forward, but Bliss stopped him with a hand on his sleeve.

"I'm truly sorry," Bliss said and took a step back to give her space.

Sage pressed, "Was he hurt?"

Bliss shook her head. "No."

The pain in the former marshal's eyes almost undid him. His daughter was lashing out and had no idea who Bliss was, but the attack was unprovoked. He moved closer to Sage. "We're doing everything we can."

The glare his daughter shot at him told him she didn't appreciate it. "What are you doing to bring my son home?"

He schooled his features. He needed to be strong to calm the situation, but he struggled to deny the fatherly instincts to offer comfort. How had things gotten so out of control that his only child could have a son and another baby on the way without telling him? Betrayal tasted bitter for this dad. Or maybe she was the one who felt betrayed by her only parent being the reason her son was abducted. "We have a team of officers searching for Wyatt and some who are looking into the old case to see if the kidnapping suspect's brother was framed."

"Why waste your time on the case? I'd think you'd use all resources to find a four-year-old kidnapped victim. Your own grandson."

"Sage, the kidnapper said if we find evidence that clears a man from death row, he'll return Wyatt."

His daughter squinted and looked to be mulling over his words. She'd matured since the last time he'd seen her—no longer a child but a woman and a mom. Beautiful.

"What makes you think the kidnapper will keep his word?" She planted her hand on her hip. "Isn't that wishful thinking and a little naive?"

"We don't know," he said. A glance at Bliss showed her leaning against the wall in the corner, her head down. No doubt the pain in her leg must be getting worse. "In case we can't locate your son but can get the kidnapper to turn him over to us, that's what we'll do."

Sage's shoulders dropped. "Okay. I can't lose him."

Zane's throat constricted. There was no greater anguish than the pain of a loved one and not being able to take it away. He wished he could gather her in his arms like he'd done when she was young and turn her hurt into unicorns and rainbows with a silly joke or a piece of candy. He simply didn't have that power anymore. By the tension radiating off her like a shrill warning, he didn't think she'd welcome the effort. "I'm sorry. Hear me now. We will bring Wyatt home."

"I appreciate that, Father. But even *you* can't promise that."

He kept from responding as his chest tightened. But

she was wrong, and she'd always called him Daddy. "The police said the kidnapper's vehicle dragged you, and you were in the hospital. Are you okay?"

"I'm fine. Mainly scrapes and bruises. I never should've let him walk beside but kept him in the cart." She rubbed her belly. "The baby wasn't injured."

"It wasn't your fault, but it's good news you weren't injured more seriously." Even though Chasity had filled him in on the abduction, he wished Sage would trust him enough to tell him more. He turned to Bliss. "I need to check in with Dryden to see if the search with the drone has produced results." As he moved toward the door, he stopped. "Oh, and, Sage, you're welcome to stay at the house."

"No, thank you. I'm staying at a hotel." Her tone was friendlier, but the words stung.

"What can I do to help?" His daughter's voice lost some of its edge. "I can't just twiddle my thumbs and do nothing."

He didn't blame her, but many times, the family slowed the search down because they questioned things or put themselves in danger.

When he hesitated, she quickly added, "Don't tell me I need to go wait at the hotel."

"I wouldn't do that."

Bliss stepped forward but left a comfortable distance. "Would you like to hang out here in the conference room? That way you'll be kept abreast of any recent developments. Officers will be coming and going, and you'll probably be bored, but it's better than being at a hotel."

Sage gave Bliss another look. "I'd like that."

"There's fresh coffee and a vending machine down

the hall. And, personally, that seat is the most comfortable in the room." Bliss pointed to the two-person sofa on the far wall.

"Thanks."

Zane added, "I'll let you know as soon as we learn anything if you'll give me your cell phone number."

She took his phone and punched the keypad.

He loved seeing his daughter again, but the distance between them was insurmountable.

The chief of police, Jason Cunningham, whisked into the room and took purposeful strides toward their small group. He was a tall, muscular man, with a deep tan and sun-bleached hair that the black uniform seemed to enhance. Nowadays, some men got artificial tans, but Jason looked to spend time outdoors. Earlier, Zane had noticed a couple of fishing trophies and a hunting picture on the wall of his office.

"Chief, can we get a statement?" a lady with a cameraman on her heels asked. "We'd like for this to be on the six o'clock news, so we don't have much time."

"Yes." He held up a finger to Zane. "Hold on. I'd like to get the public to keep an eye out for the suspect and the boy. I'll be right back."

Zane watched as the man strode with a swagger to the news lady. Sometimes law officers were excellent at their jobs but weren't much on public relations. He listened as the chief gave a description of Lawrence, Wyatt and the truck they were driving. Zane acknowledged Cunningham appeared comfortable in front of the camera.

"If you think you see the suspect, do not approach him, for he's considered dangerous. No matter how insignificant you believe the information, please let us know. Call our tip line with a message, and we'll return your call if we have questions. Lawrence Weaver's and Wyatt's photos will be posted on social media and our website. We appreciate each of you." The chief gave a decisive nod. "Let's come together as a community and bring Wyatt home."

Zane was ready to get on the road but waited until he could talk with Cunningham. As soon as the man's message was complete, he made his way over.

"I heard you took a bullet." The chief directed the comment at Bliss.

"Yes, but it caused minor damage. Mainly just annoying."

Sage scrutinized Bliss, her eyebrows arching in surprise. No doubt his daughter hadn't realized Bliss was shot while trying to rescue Wyatt.

The chief continued, "I'm glad your injuries were not more serious." Then he turned to Sage. "You're the victim's mother?"

"Yes." Her reply came out raspy.

"I want you to know we're doing everything in our power to locate your son and bring him home. I offer my condolences that this terrible situation happened." He switched his attention to Zane. "I missed the earlier briefing. Would you care to update me?"

Zane had never liked it when someone in charge slowed down investigations because they were late to the party when one of his fellow officers could bring him up to speed. Instead of voicing his irritation, he gave Cunningham a brief description of the morning's activities. "Ranger Dryden may offer more details."

The chief glanced at his cell phone, seemingly to check the time. "I appreciate it, Lieutenant. If there's anything more we can do to help, let me know. Finding your grandson is our first priority."

"Thanks." He turned to Bliss. "Are you ready?"

"Ready."

He told Sage he'd be in touch, and then he and Bliss walked out to his truck. As much as he didn't like to lean on others, he was glad the former marshal was with him.

Just as he went to open the door for her, he noticed a wet line ran on the pavement to under their car, and the strong smell of gasoline burned his nose. "Move!"

Bliss's eyes grew large as he took her hand and sprinted across the parking lot.

Boom!

Fire rained down on them as Zane tackled her to the ground.

Not again. Not only had someone taken his grandson, but this made the third time that the woman he'd practically pleaded with to help him on the case had almost gotten killed.

And if he couldn't protect her surrounded by officers, then he couldn't keep her safe anywhere.

SEVEN

Bliss's heart pounded in her chest, and pain shot through her leg. She tried to draw up, but Zane's weight kept her pinned to the ground. Heat from the explosion was suffocating. "Get off me." When he didn't respond, she asked, "Zane, are you okay?"

Voices sounded as officers filed out of the conference building.

"What?" He rolled away and leaned back on his knees. "Are you injured? Besides from your earlier gun wound, that is."

Every muscle in her body screamed with agony, but she shook her head. "I'm fine."

Ranger Dryden and Chief Cunningham made their way through the growing crowd.

Dryden asked, "Do you need an ambulance?"

Zane scooped his Stetson off the ground and shoved it back on his head. "No. Not unless I hurt Bliss's injury when I tackled her."

"I'm good." To prove it, she grasped Zane's outstretched hand and struggled to her feet, trying not to grimace. It was a failed attempt. She wasn't twenty anymore. "Ow."

Zane's gaze connected with hers, but she quickly

frowned, warning him not to mention it. She'd be fine once she got off this leg.

"What happened?" Dryden asked his boss. "Did you see anyone nearby?"

Bliss searched the group carefully.

"No." Zane explained about seeing liquid on the ground right before the explosion.

Someone had to know they would be leaving soon. Was the attacker watching? Was he in the crowd? She glanced around, but all she saw were law enforcement personnel and several cars parked in the lot next door. There was no one outside of the neighboring building— the sign read Liberty Investment Services—and no one was sitting in their vehicles that she could see. She hadn't been looking for an attack when surrounded by so many Texas Rangers and police officers.

This was going to delay searching for Wyatt even longer. She couldn't deal with that. When there was a break in the conversation, she moved closer to Zane. "While you handle this, I'm going to see if Chandler can give me a ride home so I can get my vehicle."

"Give me ten minutes to catch Dryden and the other investigators up on the little we know, and I'll go with you."

"Okay." She found Chandler, and he agreed to give them a ride. She climbed into the back of his four-door pickup, careful not to put weight on her left leg, while they waited on Zane. She didn't want to admit it, but she needed to stretch out to stop the cramping.

She wouldn't complain—no one wanted to hear whining—but her injury was killing her. The older she got, the slower she recovered. Or maybe when she was younger, she thought she was invincible. After witnessing so much death in her life, she no longer believed anyone was bulletproof.

Tucker, a beautiful bloodhound, lay beside her with his tongue hanging out. Dark brown eyes stared up at her, and she patted his head. The dog had been with her organization for several years, and she hated the thought of not seeing her team on a daily basis. But she had already made up her mind. This was her last case, and she intended to see it through until the end.

Fifteen minutes later, Zane joined them in the vehicle. The trip seemed to take extra long as she tried to relax. She only half listened to the men discuss the investigation. Since they'd been hit with multiple attacks, Zane made certain her house was clear of any dangers when they arrived.

After Chandler left, she turned to him. "Make yourself comfortable. I'm going to clean up."

"Are you okay?" Concern showed as lines creased his forehead.

"I'm exhausted and feel yucky after being in the lake and getting sand all over me. I'll think better when I'm in clean clothes." After padding back to her room, she covered her bandage with plastic wrap to keep it dry before taking a quick shower. She dressed in her field attire of khakis and a navy polo with the Bring the Children Home logo. She was careful not to bump the bullet wound. Even though the injury constantly ached, she only took half of a pain pill. Drowsiness was a side effect of the medication, and she needed to be on top of her game.

When she returned to the living room, Zane was sitting on her couch with his hands folded. Was he praying? As soon as he felt her presence, he sat up. "Are you wanting to go back out?"

"No. I'll see the case through. I already told you that."

"Not *back out*. Do you want to *go* back out? As in, stay here and rest or keep searching?"

"Oh." Her mouth lifted in a smile. "I'd love to keep looking, but my mind is running in a hundred different directions. While with the marshals, I learned my limitations. I can survive on a couple of hours of sleep, but I can't go less than that."

"I understand. I feel much the same way. But…"

"Let me guess. You can rest when your grandson is home again."

He ran his fingers through his hair. "Yeah. I suppose you're right. Until we get another solid lead, I'm probably better off getting some shut-eye instead of searching blind."

"Exactly." Her thigh continued to throb. She moved past him and sat on the sofa so she could put up her leg. Her furniture wasn't as plush as some, but it power-reclined, which, at the moment, was calling her name.

He took the other end of the couch. "I had no idea Sage had a son or was expecting. I've really made a mess of things, haven't I?"

"Nothing that can't be undone." She laid her hand on his shirtsleeve, the muscle in his bicep solid and warm. "But this could be the catalyst that brings you all back together."

"I disagree. Did you see the disdain in the look she gave me?" He shook his head. "She hates me, and I've given her good reason."

"I have a hard time believing that. Try not to take

her distant attitude too seriously. I don't know your daughter, but she's young and a mom, and her child has been abducted. Patience. Be here for her. I'll say a prayer for healing."

His gaze searched hers, like he was considering her words. "Thanks for saying that, Bliss. I hope you're right."

She sighed. "I had more experience in the rebellion department than I ever told you about." At his raised eyebrow, she went on to explain. "My anger was directed at my mom rather than my dad, but it was the same emotions. I'd always been a daddy's girl, spending time with him at the shooting range, helping haul hay and playing chess. He was my hero, but he'd died in the line of duty as a US marshal when I was fourteen. Mom didn't want me to be in the dangerous job of law enforcement. She even applied to several colleges who had good accounting programs for me behind my back. Can you imagine me being an accountant?"

He shook his head. "Not really. But I understand your mom's concern."

"Me too. Now. When I confronted her, she insisted if I gave it a try, I'd enjoy a quiet and stable career while still having a husband and kids. Looking back, she was probably right. At that time, I believed she wanted to erase my dad from my memory, like he never existed."

"I remember you talking about your dad. Even though I never knew him, I realize you two had been close."

If Bliss could only undo her juvenile ways, she would. She'd been stubborn and didn't want to be told what to do. Looking back, she understood her mom was petrified of losing her only daughter and had been struggling with the death of her spouse, just as Zane was. The cost had been permanent.

When she glanced back at the ranger, his expression showed strain. The room closed in as she realized how near she'd been sitting to him, her hand still gripping his arm. Like touching a hot stove, she jerked away from the searing contact. "Sorry."

To her chagrin, he simply looked at her, but she couldn't tell what he was thinking.

Feeling like a teenager, she scolded herself for acting silly. She hadn't dated since Adam died. Occasionally, she went out with a group of coworkers or friends, including men, but nothing that led to a relationship. It wasn't for lack of being asked. Her mission had been to find Mitchell, and that made no time for romance.

Things needed to stay that way. Who could think of love when there was a child out there wanting his mama and in the hands of a criminal and would-be killer?

Sometimes it'd be nice to have someone to come home to, to share long walks in the fall or to see a movie with. Even to argue over the remote or where to go out to eat. The thoughts bubbled from the deep recesses of her mind, but as always, she quickly shoved them back into place. The only constant in her life was the loss of those she loved.

"What did I do wrong?"

She looked at him. "I don't know. Teens are hard to figure. I'm certain it was her mom's death in the accident."

"Not with her. With you."

She swallowed. She didn't want to go there. Not now. At her hesitancy, he continued. "I get you had a job opportunity, but why break our engagement suddenly without calling or staying in touch? You ignored my phone calls."

She was too ashamed to tell him the real reason. Would he be able to forgive her if he learned the truth?

Zane watched as an array of emotions crossed her face. What was going through her mind? "I'm that bad, huh? You left and then Sage took off."

"It's not like that. There was a lot going on back then. Things I couldn't deal with." She paused and glanced at him like there was something she wanted to say.

"What is it?"

She glanced down and fidgeted with her hands—something she never did.

What did that mean? He rubbed his hands down his jeans as frustration built. "I'm trying to understand what I did. I thought you and I were on the right track. We were planning our wedding and future together when you received an offer to train for the US Marshals. I get that it was a dream job…" She stared at him as he tried to form his thoughts into words. "But why not try to work things out? Sage was the same way. Her mom's death hit her hard, and we were struggling. *I* was struggling. She kept telling me to get off her back. So, when she walked away, I didn't go after her to drag her home, even though the father in me wanted to. I gave her space like I thought she wanted."

"You didn't come after me, either."

Her statement sent a knife to his heart. "I thought you wanted nothing to do with me. Are you saying you would've come back if I had gone after you?"

"Maybe." Bliss shrugged. "I guess I'd watched too

many romances back during those days. I was dealing with…things. I'd hoped you'd come riding up on your white horse."

"You've said twice that you were dealing with things. What things?"

"Nothing." She drew a deep breath. "It was personal."

He took in her nervous movements and noted she wouldn't look at him. "Did I do or say something wrong? I was younger back then, more impatient."

"Please." She glanced at him, her eyes glistening. "I don't want to talk about it now. All of that is in the past."

She'd wanted him to come after her. Of course, he should've, but he was reeling from her up and moving to Atlanta. His feelings were hurt, and he hadn't known how to deal with that. His first instinct was to get mad and pretend not to care.

Her shoulder lifted. "I didn't realize it then, but I was missing my dad. We were planning a wedding, and he wasn't going to be a part of it. I was following in his steps, and it felt like neither my mom nor you supported me."

His gaze went to the floor. Had Sage felt the same way? That he didn't care enough to come after her? He'd never told his daughter he'd had an investigator keep track of where she was staying and where she was working for the first year. He assumed that would've furthered the divide between them.

And he'd made Bliss feel the same way? It wasn't true. He had wanted to go after her, but she wasn't even taking his calls. He couldn't very well demand she return to Texas. He'd hoped she would return on her own.

"I had a lot going on and could've handled it differ-

ently. That's why I say give Sage time to come around."
She put the footrest down on the sofa and climbed to
her feet, then stood a moment. "I'm going to lie down
for an hour or two. Will you be fine?"

He stood and held out his arm to assist her.

"You stop that." She waved him off. "I've got this.
Make yourself at home."

He watched her walk away with a stiff gait and
heard her bedroom door shut. What *things* had she been
dealing with? Why couldn't she confide in him? While
she was out of the room, he called Dryden. "Have you
learned anything?"

"Not yet. There were no security cameras on that
portion of the parking lot. We're checking the investment firm next door to see if they picked up anyone
near your truck."

"Good. What about the tip hotline?"

Dryden sighed. "Like normal. We're getting a lot of
messages now and trying to sift through them so we
can prioritize. We've been inquiring if anyone saw anything suspicious the few minutes before the explosion,
but nothing so far."

"Okay. Keep asking around."

"You know it."

After he hung up, he paced the floor. Someone had
to have seen something, even if they didn't realize it.
The chief had walked in not long after Sage. Those
were the last two people Zane noticed entering the
building, but he'd been talking and could've easily
missed the perpetrator coming inside. He also tried to
remember if anyone had left, but he'd been too preoccupied with conversation.

Texas Ranger Jax O'Neill had sent Zane a message

earlier that he'd located Stuart Simpson—Sean Weaver's roommate, who'd moved out three weeks prior to the shooting. They were pursuing several leads, and any of them could bring them to the person who set up Sean Weaver.

The timeline was simply too tight to do a good job of following up on all possibilities. And like Sage had said, there was nothing to say Lawrence wouldn't change his mind and kill the boy.

Zane had had little to eat or drink all day, and he decided to see if Bliss had milk or tea to drink. On his way to the kitchen, he noticed a lamp on in an office. He stopped in the doorway and took in several awards and photos on the wall for Bring the Children Home Project. When his gaze went to her desk, his chest tightened. A photo of Bliss, Adam and a boy caught his attention. All three of them were smiling and appeared happy. News of Bliss's marriage had traveled through the grapevine, and he'd looked up their wedding announcement online. By then, he was dating Vivian seriously. He'd never quite gotten over Bliss but had chalked it up to first love.

"What are you looking for?"

Zane flinched as she startled him. "I was walking by and noticed your awards."

Her gaze went from him to the family photo on the desk. "I got back up because I wanted to offer you something to eat and drink before I fall asleep."

"Thanks. I'd love a glass of milk and a sandwich or anything easy."

He stepped out of the room, and he noted she closed the office door behind him. He hadn't been snooping. Or maybe he had just a little.

She made him a turkey on rye and poured him some milk. He sat at the bar in the kitchen. She sliced an apple and eased onto the stool beside him.

His stomach growled as he took a bite, and he smiled. "I guess I was hungrier than I realized."

"Me too." She crunched on the slice of fruit. "Please don't feel the need to stay here with me. If you receive a tip or want to check on something, go. I would do the same."

"I wouldn't leave without telling you." He looked at her. "You've done a lot of good with your organization."

"Thanks."

He expected her to say more, but she continued to nibble on the apple. Her annoyed expression hadn't changed much through the years, and he almost laughed. "Don't you believe me?"

Her shoulders slumped. "I do. But I can't think about it right now."

Or talk about it, he surmised. As he finished his sandwich and swallowed the last bit of milk, he remained quiet. He watched as she got up from the bar and wiped down the counter. If he'd learned anything these past few years, it was that if you didn't say what was on your mind, you may never get the chance. "If it's any consolation, you've helped reunite more families than anyone I know. You're the best in the business. I'm sorry I wasn't here for you a few months ago when you received the news of your son."

While she stared at him, he said, "The food hit the spot. Good night." He put his dishes in the sink and walked out, not giving her time to refute the claim. A few seconds later, her bedroom door closed.

She was struggling with the loss of her son, but it

was important she knew how crucial her work was to others. He prayed his grandson's story was one with a happy ending.

Hopefully, Bliss got some rest. Instinct told him the dangers were only going to get worse.

EIGHT

Bliss awoke with a start. She glanced at the clock. It read two thirty-three. Almost four hours of sleep, which was twice as much as she anticipated. She tossed the throw aside, slid on her shoes and walked out to the living room.

Empty.

"Zane?" She padded through the house and found him in the dining area.

"What are you doing?"

"I was on the phone and didn't want to wake you. I received a call from Dryden."

She prayed it was good news.

"He's about to talk to Stuart Simpson—Sean Weaver's former roommate. We're hoping to learn more of Sean's acquaintances before the shooting, or if Simpson is connected. Anything that might lead us to the killer."

"That's encouraging." She was more concerned with finding Wyatt, though. If they could find evidence that Sean was framed, that still didn't guarantee the boy would be found.

"Don't be disappointed. They're still going through the tips. There's a couple that look promising. O'Neill is checking one where a female caller claimed her next-door neighbor had a young boy with him. And there was another sighting from someone in Hodge County that described a man with Lawrence's description scouting around an abandoned hunting cabin. I'll be investigating that lead, if you want to join me."

"You know I do. Let me grab my things." A few minutes later, she had her gun and pocket-size purse. Even though she knew the tip lines had many calls that didn't pan out, sometimes a caller had seen something that led them to the right place. "I'm ready. Are we taking my SUV?"

"The Rangers dropped off a replacement truck last night at the community center. We can swing by and pick it up on the way out of town."

"That'll work." They hurried to get into her Tahoe. "Do you know who owns the cabin?"

"Yeah. An elderly lady by the last name of Abernathy. She lives in Dallas and purchased the land eighteen years ago for investment purposes. Over the years, she leased the place to hunters."

Bliss nodded. So a number of people could be familiar with the property. It wasn't uncommon for hunters to bring their friends or coworkers for a weekend getaway. As she drove to the center, Zane talked on the phone, evidently gaining more details. Once they switched vehicles, he took over the driving.

She found herself leaning forward, eager to check out the location.

As they entered the next county, other vehicles were nonexistent. They turned off a rural highway onto a paved road. As they headed deeper off the beaten path, she couldn't help but notice there were hardly any homes out this way. One modest brick house sat in the trees, and then they went several miles without passing another. Potholes littered the way, probably made worse by the recent rains. Zane took a left at a T in the road. Only pastures and a few cornfields were in the area. "This seems like a perfect place to commit a crime and not get caught."

"I was thinking the same thing."

"Are you certain you're on the right path?" She had seen no homes for several miles.

"If my GPS is correct, the place is up ahead."

You have arrived at your destination. The words lit up on his phone.

He put on his brakes and scanned the area. "Do you see anything?"

"Nothing." Weeds lined the ditches and barbed wire fencing surrounded the pastures.

He eased forward and then stopped at a culvert.

Grass overtook the dirt drive, and Bliss hoped his truck wouldn't get stuck. "This is the only entrance, but it doesn't look like there's a house around here."

"I agree, but let's check it out. I'll get the gate."

The sagging barbed wire entrance was similar to many pastures all over the Texas countryside.

Zane got back in and pulled up to a faint, rough trail, the truck bouncing with each hit. In a couple of places, he had to floor it to get through substantial mudholes, but he soon topped a hill. The headlights landed on two old shipping containers that lined up side by side, like they were connected. Plywood covered the front door and the only visible window. Trees surrounded the place. He eased forward a little more.

"They called this a hunting cabin?" Bliss said.

"Yeah." He put the truck into Park. "This is as close as we get. We'll have to tramp through the mud the rest of the way. Metal containers make good hunting cabins, but I'm surprised the caller didn't specify the type of house."

"I agree." She sat up straight. "I can't imagine who saw a man and child in this secluded area. Almost had to be a farmer. This would be the perfect hiding place. It's off the beaten path and sits back away from the road. A person could have lights on inside, and no one could see it. The good thing is he shouldn't be able to notice our headlights, either."

"Hopefully, they're sleeping. Lawrence has been running for two days." He leaned forward. "I don't see a vehicle. Do you?"

"No. But there could be one around back."

"True, but there should be tracks. Unless there's a different access road." He opened his door and stepped out. "I'm going in. Are you with me?"

"Do you have to ask?"

"I wouldn't blame you if you remained in the truck."

She sighed. "I think you say these things just to aggravate me."

He chuckled and then sobered as he scoped out the place. He pointed right and whispered, "I'm going that way."

"Okay. I'll check out the south side of the house." With her gun in one hand and her flashlight in the other, Bliss kept an eye out as she hurried down the tree line. Water saturated the ground, and mud was everywhere. There was no avoiding getting her boots dirty. An owl hooted in the distance. Branches swayed in the wind.

As she made it to the front corner of the rusty container, she noticed plywood didn't cover a little section of the grime-covered window. She glimpsed in and stood on her tiptoes while cupping her hands to her face. Still nothing.

There were no other windows on this side, so she proceeded to the back to check out the backyard. Zane came her way. Keeping her voice down, she asked, "Did you see anyone?"

"No. And no vehicle or tracks."

"I wonder if we have the wrong address." She continued to shine her flashlight around.

"We won't know until we look inside the place."

"I'm with you." As she dodged the larger puddles, suddenly a footprint reflected in the light. Her hand shot out. "Wait."

Zane halted.

"Is that yours?"

He shook his head. "I didn't walk across this area."

She continued toward the structure, careful not to step on the tracks. They stopped at the steel back door—the only access not covered with plywood.

Zane held his finger in the air and mouthed, "Follow me."

She nodded.

He swung the door open. "Texas Ranger Adcock." With his weapon ready, he walked through the place, pausing at doorways before entering.

Bliss kept an eye on the floor to check for footprints to warn her if anyone had been inside. A musty odor was whipped up by a breeze that blew through the house, indicating either a window or door was open. She stayed five feet back from the lieutenant to give him ample room in case someone jumped out. The two-bedroom, one-bathroom building didn't take long to clear.

He lowered his gun. "Doesn't look like anyone's been here recently."

Disappointment that they'd run into another dead end hit her. "I still wonder if we're in the right place. Or maybe the person who left the tip gave the wrong address. The caller said 'cabin,' which makes me question if there's a house nearby."

"Could be. Looks like it's been a while since anyone stayed here."

"I noticed that, too. Besides the old potbellied stove and a twin bed on a wooden pallet, there is little other furniture." A few pictures hung on the wall, and one showed a black-and-white shot of an older couple in front of a Model T. "Do you recognize anyone in the photo?"

"No." He snapped a picture of it on his cell phone. "Dryden had reported Abernathy owned the property, and hopefully, she can provide us a list of people who used the cabin."

She nodded. "That would be helpful. Have you ever been to a hunting cabin or lodge that didn't have photos or heads of their latest kill?"

"I'm sure you remember I'm not a big hunter. But you're right. This doesn't seem like a hunting cabin, at least not anymore."

Frustration ate at her, like something escaped their attention. "Where to now?" A glance back at him showed a strange look on his face. "What?"

He shook his head. "I don't know. The place looks familiar for some reason. Anyway, unless one of my rangers has found something promising, I say we return to the community center and take the next tip. If you have a better suggestion…"

"I agree. It feels like we're at the wrong place." She headed through the tiny kitchen toward the back of the house. When she turned the knob, she almost face-planted into the door where they had come in. "It's locked."

Zane stepped around her. "I can do it."

She moved out of his way, even though she was ca-pable of telling if a door would open.

He yanked on it, but the mass of steel didn't budge. Their gazes connected.

"Let me knock out a window."

Her heart sank into the pit of her stomach as she watched him kick the plywood covering the living room window. The loud bang reverberated through the house, and his boot struck the plywood again and again.

Someone had locked them in this storage container in the middle of nowhere. They had to get out of here. She hurried to the other window and kicked using the heel of her boot. Pain shot through her, but they couldn't just sit here. Time was running out.

Zane looked over at Bliss, his breath coming in pants. "Don't hurt yourself. I can do this."

He strode through the other container to the back bedroom. The plyboard didn't cover all of this window, so he gave it a good kick. *Crack*. Encouraged, he de-livered another quick blow with his boot.

As he continued slamming into the covering, warn-ing bells went off in his head. Someone had locked them in. What if they started a fire? The container mostly being metal would give them some protection, but the floor was wood, along with the framing of the joint between the containers. Just the thought of them being trapped made him move faster. He could shoot a few rounds into the plywood, but that would only make a few small holes.

Bam. Bam.

"Zane. Someone's on the roof."

He stopped working. Specks of white floated to the dust-covered boards as the paint flaked off the ceiling. Pointing his gun upward, he waited. No one should fire a weapon without seeing their target, but chances were the person planned to harm them. The bullet would certainly ricochet. Still…

Something fell out of the chimney and clattered to the floor. Fog filled the air. And then another one clanked to the floor.

Bliss yelled, "Gas!"

He pulled the trigger. Footsteps pounded across the roof, and a loud crash indicated they had slid or tumbled off. "Cover your face."

The metal makeshift home was filling with gas quickly.

His eyes burned as he hurried to the bedroom window that was already cracked. He unloaded his weapon into the plywood. Dizziness caused him to stagger. The agent must be some kind of incapacitating gas.

Bliss appeared beside him. "Get down!"

But he continued to pelt the window with gunfire. He was barely aware of Bliss punching numbers into her cell phone.

He pulled the trigger, but the clip was empty. Desperate to escape the house, he slammed into the window with his shoulder. The board split with a loud crack, and then his head was spinning. He put his hand out to catch himself, but as he swayed, he couldn't stop himself from hitting the floor.

His world grew dark no matter how hard he concentrated on staying awake. If he passed out, Bliss would be vulnerable to whoever had tossed the gas into the structure.

NINE

Bliss woke with a pounding headache. Cold and grit pressed against her cheek. Her eyes blinked open as her brain fought to clear the cobwebs.

She pushed herself to a sitting position on the wooden floor and looked around. Where was she?

She and Zane had gone to check out a tip. Panic slammed into her as she glanced about for him. He wasn't in the narrow room. Fighting dizziness, she struggled to her feet and hurried into a bedroom. Her gaze landed on the cowboy figure on the floor.

"Zane." She knelt by his side. Slivers of sunlight shone through the cracks of the shipping container. How long had they been out? She gave his jaw a gentle slap. "Wake up, Zane."

Gruff murmurs came from his lips, and he grimaced.

"You need to wake up." She shook his shoulder and then glanced up at the hole in the plywood. "We need fresh air."

He rubbed his hand on his forehead and groaned. "My head is killing me."

"Can you stand?"

"What happened?" He squinted in confusion.

"Someone was on the roof and dropped two canisters of something into the room—one that failed to go off."

"I remember." He pushed to his feet and stood beside the opening in the plywood. After a moment, as realization dawned, he stepped back. "Get over here."

"I'm fine." She waved him away and glanced at her phone. "We've been out for a couple of hours."

"Let me call Dryden and inform him of what's going on."

While Zane called the ranger, she walked through the structure again for a place that might be easier to escape. But after a thorough search, she didn't see a simpler way out.

Zane shook his head. "There's nothing new to report. We need to get back to the center."

"Looks like that window is the best way out."

He strode to the twin mattress that was positioned on several pallets and grabbed a slat. With a mighty kick, the board came away in his hands. Using it like a baseball bat, he swung at the window.

Several more hits, and the crack grew into a big enough gap they could crawl through. He shoved the rest of the covering out of the way and crawled out the window feetfirst.

"You're an impatient man."

"Yeah." He grinned up at her. "Come on."

"Give me a second." She grabbed the frame and squirmed through until she could sit on the ledge and roll over. With his hands on her waist, she let herself down to the ground.

"Are you okay?" His brown eyes stared into hers. She came up to his chest, and with him staring down, the cleft in his chin was at eye level.

She would've taken a step back to give them distance, but the container wall was too close. "I'm fine."

"You don't have a headache?"

"I do, but it's not as bad as when I first awoke." She glanced away, breaking eye contact with him. The lieutenant's six-foot-three height towered over her—something she'd always liked when they were dating. He had that rugged man thing going for him, and his size had made him stand out in most crowds. But she wasn't a young, impressionable girl anymore, so she stepped around him.

Being more mature, she'd learned it took more than good looks to get her attention. She caught a glimpse of him in the corner of her eye. Not that his handsome looks were a bad thing. She called over her shoulder, "Is your head hurting?"

"It is, but I'll live."

When she was a distance from him, she turned back to him. "Do you think the person who dropped the canister was trying to kill us? Or just trying to keep us detained?"

"Detained," he said with confidence.

"How can you be so sure?"

He nodded. "Take a look."

She turned around and saw his truck with two flat tires. "Oh, you've got to be kidding me."

"Let me get a tire shop to get us going again." His jaw clenched as he scrolled on his cell phone.

As he talked to the place, she trekked over to the truck and leaned against the front of it. Her gaze went from the shipping container to the driveway until it disappeared in the trees. The road couldn't be seen from here, which meant no one could've witnessed a man and child at the hunting cabin. They could've seen Lawrence going in or out of the gate. But...

Zane strode her way. "Makes me question the reason someone had to trap us out here. Were they hoping the execution would be carried out before we learned the truth?"

"I was just thinking about that." She explained about being unable to see the road from here, which meant whoever left the tip had either been lying or had seen Lawrence at the gate. But they had to know about the cabin.

He shoved his hands into his pockets. "You're right. Then whoever the caller is must be hoping for Sean Weaver's execution."

"What if the tip came from Lawrence, and he was the one who dropped the canisters?"

Zane looked at her. "What would be the purpose?"

"Because he has Wyatt hidden in a place that might be easy to find, and he wants to move him?"

Zane squinted. "I don't know... We only have until Friday night. I'd think he'd rather save his brother than worry about keeping Wyatt from us."

"You're probably right. It was just a thought. How long until the tire guy shows up?"

"About an hour." He pushed away from the truck. "And since we have a little time, I'm going to scout around now that it's daylight to see if we can learn more about last night's visitor."

Bliss watched him survey the land surrounding the structure. Her head only mildly throbbed at the moment. Sleepiness still tugged at her. Partly from exhaustion and partly the incapacitating gas—whatever kind had been used. Just over two more days until Sean's execution.

And then what?

Would Lawrence really kill an innocent child? There was no way to know for certain, but she wasn't willing to bet Wyatt's life on it.

Frustration bit at Zane as he explored around the containers. Finding Wyatt again before the execution deadline was not looking good. He'd worked plenty of investigations where there was little evidence to go on, or the stakes were high. But this one hit home.

What did someone have to gain by detaining them? They had to be missing something. He kept returning to the Sean Weaver case. Texas Ranger Brendan Hale had taken the lead with the investigation since Zane was new to the team. Now, sixteen years later, Hale was still with the Rangers but had talked about retiring next summer.

Was this the missing piece? Zane didn't like going behind his superior's back, so he punched in his number on his cell phone.

"This is Brewer. Have you found your grandson?"

"No, Captain." Zane gave him a quick update of the tip that led them to the hunting place in the boonies.

"So, you think the message was a setup?"

"Yes, I do. And time is running out."

"What can I do for you?"

He drew a deep breath. "I keep going round and round with who could've planted evidence."

"*If* someone planted evidence."

"If…" His gut told him Lawrence was telling the truth about that, but the captain would want proof. "I helped with that investigation, and I keep reviewing the details in my mind. It was a solid case. I was new to the

Rangers, but I'd worked several homicides with state troopers before then, so it's not like I was a rookie." He took another deep breath. "I'd like an investigator to look at Ranger Hale."

"Adcock, I've already had Spears pull the Weaver case and Hale's report."

Zane's mind swirled. Looking at the original files would be normal protocol. "Did you find anything?"

"The documents are in order, and there's nothing to make me suspect foul play. Is there anything more I should be aware of?"

Brewer required his men to be honest and shoot straight. Not to be careless with accusations, but he expected his rangers to express their concerns. "If Hale had framed Weaver, he wouldn't be sloppy in filling out the paperwork. He was my mentor back then, and I remember he had sought out professional help for a gambling problem. He's one of the best lawmen I've ever worked with, and he emphasized following the book. But…"

"Are you suggesting he sold drugs to support his gambling habit?"

"No, I'm not. But I think it's worth digging deeper."

"I'll look into it. And, Zane, I hope you're wrong."

"Me too."

When he disconnected, he turned around to see Bliss staring at him.

"You believe another ranger might have framed Sean?"

He frowned. "I hadn't meant for you to overhear that."

Her lips flattened into a straight line.

"I feel bad for even suggesting it," he was quick to add. "But all suspects must be checked out."

"Who was it again?" She crossed her arms.

"Ranger Hale."

"I've heard the name before, but I don't believe I've ever worked with him on a case. I heard you mention gambling on the phone."

He pushed his Stetson up on his head. Next time, he'd make certain she wasn't around to overhear his conversation. Hale had even been the one who gave Zane a recommendation when he applied for the position of lieutenant. "It was many years ago, when I first started working with the Rangers. Hale was a private sort who didn't share much personal information, so he must've hit rock bottom to admit his struggle and even told our lieutenant about it at the time."

"I've heard many rangers' names over the years, but some have since been promoted or retired. Was Brewer the lieutenant at the time?"

"Not Brewer. It was Lieutenant Calderon. He retired a couple of years after that, so you might not remember him."

"The name doesn't sound familiar."

He watched her and wondered how well she'd kept up with the rangers. And him. Had she known he and Sage had a falling-out before he called her? "To let you know, Captain Brewer had already looked into his file, but he agreed to look deeper."

"We don't have much time. I'll ask Josie Hunt to help investigate, too."

Zane's eyes narrowed. "No one wants this case solved as bad as me, so feel free."

"Unless it's Sean Weaver." Her hand covered her

mouth. "Sorry. That slipped out. I realize you have a lot to lose."

He shook his head. "I'm not that sensitive, Bliss."

"Still. It was thoughtless of me. Have you found anything around this place?"

"Not yet."

"Want to check out that shed back there?" She pointed to a run-down wooded structure that was barely visible in the overgrowth.

"Why not? We should still have a few minutes before the mechanic shows up." As they made their way through the Johnsongrass and mud, he kept an eye out for snakes, but as he trekked into deeper brush, it was the poison oak that gained his attention. He pointed to a three-leaf culprit. "Careful. Don't get that stuff on you."

"Oh. I'm glad you warned me."

They exchanged glances, and she gave him a knowing look.

On their first date, he'd taken her to the lake on the Fourth of July weekend. They'd talked after class beforehand and had met a few times with other people from the police academy. There were only a handful of females in the program, but he and Bliss had hit it off immediately. When he'd finally gotten up the courage to ask her out, she'd turned him down. Three times. Not to be deterred, he tried again, and she finally agreed. The beach was crowded, and Zane had moved their blanket back close to the trees to give them some privacy while they watched the fireworks. They'd shared a kiss that night. Two days later, her skin broke out in red patches, and in another couple of days, she was covered bad enough to warrant a trip to her doctor.

Awkwardness hung in the air at the memory.

He never was one to tiptoe around a subject. "I assume you don't go near the poisonous plants anymore."

The corner of her mouth lifted. "Nope. Learned my lesson well that day."

Did her comment carry a jab to mean more than the poison oak?

She laughed. "Don't look so serious, Lieutenant."

He was glad they could laugh about their past relationship. It'd been years, so it would be uncomfortable if they couldn't,

The first thing he noticed when he entered the opening of the shed were the leaning metal shelves that were full of camouflage gear. From hooded coats and face masks to tents.

A deer feeder rested against the wall, and multiple boxes covered an old Formica dining table. Fishing poles were stored in the rafters above, and several ice chests were stacked on top of each other.

"Looks like this place was used for hunting after all." Bliss glanced around.

"Yeah." Zane stepped to the table and flipped open the first container. Multiple boxes of bullets stared back at him.

She picked up a cartridge and twirled it between her fingers. "This doesn't seem like a safe place to store ammunition. Kids or anyone could easily come upon this shed."

"I was thinking the same thing." A Winchester rifle leaned against the wall. Who left a good gun out in the open?

Zane's cell phone dinged. He read the text message before looking at her. "The tire repair guy is here."

"Finally." As Bliss walked by the table, she gasped.

"What is it?" He glanced back to see what had caused the reaction.

"I think the caller was the person who left the present for us at Lawrence's house." She pointed to a wooden crate.

A grenade.

They stared at each other.

"I'll call Dryden to see if we can get the bomb squad out here to check if those are live. And then we need to track down the person who left that tip."

"Yeah. This may be our first big break."

"Is it? Or a diversion." He looked at her. "Why would the guy who planted a grenade lead us to the location where the explosives were stored?"

TEN

Bliss propped her foot up on the edge of a cardboard box of files to ease the pain in her leg. After the technician changed their tires, the bomb squad showed up. Much to her consternation, the grenades were live and, since they were too dangerous to transport, were detonated on-site.

Just the thought of someone accidentally stumbling upon those made her nauseous.

Instead of returning to the community center, she'd ask Zane to drop her at her office at the Bring the Children Home Project. There were simply too many people coming and going with different agencies, and she craved the quiet of her own space to think.

Zane's question kept replaying through her mind. Did the person who contrived the grenade to go off when the cellar door opened also leave the message on the tip line? Or was this another setup to transfer blame to either the landowner or one of the hunters who'd leased the property?

Thinking about it gave her a headache. She squirmed in her office chair, trying unsuccessfully to get comfortable.

Josie Hunt stopped at her door, carrying a tumbler.

Faint circles formed under her eyes. "Can I get you a cup of coffee?"

"I would love some."

"One black cup coming your way." A minute later, she was back and put the drink on her desk.

"Thank you, Josie."

"Oh, and Kennedy called earlier." The investigator cringed for being the bearer of bad news. "She wants to talk to you later."

Kennedy Boone was the team's psychologist who offered counseling to the families of abducted children and to all team members who needed it. She'd been after Bliss to visit ever since she'd learned of the discovery of Mitchell's remains. Bliss had been putting it off.

"Thanks, Josie. I'll give her a call after this is over. How's the investigation going?"

The athletically built brunette leaned against the door frame. "Frustrating, although chasing rabbit trails often can be. Lawrence wasn't one to post about his life online. Digging for information to see where else he might have taken Wyatt is daunting. Nothing unusual has turned up on Ranger Hale, either. You mentioned he had a gambling problem previously, but his credit has been excellent for the past ten years. No suspicious bank accounts or loans. Even a check into his family came back clean. I realize that doesn't mean he didn't have financial trouble sixteen years ago, but there's no red flags in recent times."

"What about the interviews with Ike Harris's connections?"

She shook her head and sighed. "We've only been able to track down two relatives—Ike's widow and his

YOU pick your books –
WE pay for everything.

You get up to FOUR new books and a Mystery Gift...
absolutely FREE!

Total retail value: Over $20!

Dear Reader,

Your opinions are important to us. So if you'll participate in our fast and free "One Minute" Survey, YOU can pick up to four wonderful books that WE pay for when you try the Harlequin Reader Service!

As a leading publisher of women's fiction, we'd love to hear from you. That's why we promise to reward you for completing our survey.

IMPORTANT: Please complete the survey and return it. We'll send your Free Books and a Free Mystery Gift right away. And we pay for shipping and handling too! ← *We pay for EVERYTHING!*

Try **Love Inspired® Romance Larger-Print** and get 2 books and fall in love with inspirational romances that take you on an uplifting journey of faith, forgiveness and hope.

Try **Love Inspired® Suspense Larger-Print** and get 2 books where courage and optimism unite in stories of faith and love in the face of danger.

Or TRY BOTH!

Thank you again for participating in our "One Minute" Survey. It really takes just a minute (or less) to complete the survey... and your free books and gift will be well worth it!

If you continue with your subscription, you can look forward to curated monthly shipments of brand-new books from your selected series, always at a discount off the cover price! Plus you can cancel any time. So don't miss out, return your One Minute Survey today to get your Free books.

Pam Powers

"One Minute" Survey

GET YOUR FREE BOOKS AND A FREE GIFT!

✓ Complete this Survey ✓ Return this survey

1 Do you try to find time read every day?

☐ YES ☐ NO

2 Do you prefer books which reflect Christian values?

☐ YES ☐ NO

3 Do you enjoy having books delivered to your home?

☐ YES ☐ NO

4 Do you find a Larger Print size easier on your eyes?

☐ YES ☐ NO

YES! I have completed the above "One Minute" Survey. Please send me my Free Books and a Free Mystery Gift (worth over $20 retail). I understand that I am under no obligation to buy anything, as explained on the back of this card.

☐ **Love Inspired®
Romance
Larger-Print**
122/322 CTI G29C

☐ **Love Inspired®
Suspense
Larger-Print**
107/307 CTI G29C

☐ **BOTH**
122/322 & 107/307
CTI G29E

FIRST NAME

LAST NAME

ADDRESS

APT.#

CITY

STATE/PROV.

ZIP/POSTAL CODE

EMAIL ☐ Please check this box if you would like to receive newsletters and promotional emails from Harlequin Enterprises ULC and its affiliates. You can unsubscribe anytime.

LI/LIS-1123-OM_123ST

⟨H⟩HARLEQUIN® Reader Service —**Here's how it works:**

Accepting your 2 free books and free gift (gift valued at approximately $10.00 retail) places you under no obligation to buy anything. You may keep the books and gift and return the shipping statement marked "cancel." If you do not cancel, approximately one month later we'll send you 6 more books from each series you have chosen, and bill you at our low, subscribers-only discount price. Love Inspired® Romance Larger-Print books and Love Inspired® Suspense Larger-Print books consist of 6 books each month and cost just $6.49 each in the U.S. or $6.74 each in Canada. That is a savings of at least 13% off the cover price. It's quite a bargain! Shipping and handling is just 50¢ per book in the U.S. and $1.25 per book in Canada*. You may return any shipment at our expense and cancel at any time by contacting customer service — or you may continue to receive monthly shipments at our low, subscribers-only discount price plus shipping and handling.

▲ If offer card is missing write to: Harlequin Reader Service, P.O. Box 1341, Buffalo, NY 14240-8531 or visit www.ReaderService.com ▲

BUSINESS REPLY MAIL
FIRST-CLASS MAIL   PERMIT NO. 717   BUFFALO, NY

POSTAGE WILL BE PAID BY ADDRESSEE

HARLEQUIN READER SERVICE
PO BOX 1341
BUFFALO NY 14240-8571

NO POSTAGE
NECESSARY
IF MAILED
IN THE
UNITED STATES

son. Chasity paid a visit to both of them. They sang Ike's praises and denied he planted drugs on anyone, even against his ex-wife's boyfriend—the one that was caught on camera. After Ike lost his position with the dispatch office, he worked several jobs but didn't stay at any of them for very long. Most former coworkers barely remember him."

Bliss rolled her eyes. "That sounds about right."

"I talked with Officer Richards at the center. He said calls to the tip line have slowed to a trickle."

"I was afraid of that." She tapped her fingers on her desk. "You're free to go home and get rest. You look tired."

"I don't mind, boss. I'm waiting on a phone call and wouldn't be able to relax anyway."

Bliss had been busy with her own grief the past several months, but it hadn't escaped her attention that her competent investigator had been distracted of late. Josie was a good team player, but when it came to her personal life, she was a closed book. As far as Bliss knew, Josie didn't have a boyfriend or much kinfolk nearby. Except for a grandfather, family was one thing she never mentioned, even when she'd taken a bullet a few months ago and was in the hospital and rehab for weeks. "If you need to talk, I'm here."

"Thanks." She shot her a quick smile and disappeared down the hall.

Bliss stared at the empty doorway for a moment. What had she missed while she'd been busy grieving the loss of Mitchell?

Her gaze fell on the file on her desk. Even though everything was online now, there was something stimulating about the touch of paper that got her thinking juices flowing better than scrolling on a computer.

The report from Ranger Hale detailed all the evidence clearly, along with photos of the crime scene. According to the report, the gun that killed Officer Larson was lying under Sean Weaver's hand like he'd dropped it when hit. The pictures showed the officer lay in the doorway between the living room and kitchen—his head in the living room as if he'd been entering the kitchen when shot and fell back.

The coroner wrote that Larson's time of death was between 7:00 and 8:00 p.m. Sean had clocked out at work at two minutes past seven from the factory, which would've given him plenty of opportunity to commit the murder.

The next-door neighbor heard two gunshots seconds apart and called 9-1-1 at 7:47. Two Liberty police officers, Montoya and Guerra, arrived nine minutes later at 7:56, when they discovered both Officer Larson and Sean Weaver with gunshot wounds. Two bullet casings were found in the kitchen. Larson was dead at the scene, and Sean was alive and rushed to the hospital. Under the Additional Notes section, Hale stated another bullet was discovered by an investigator in the kitchen wall.

Bliss glanced through the detailed photos of the scene. Everything seemed to line up except for the neighbor only hearing two shots, but there were three bullets discharged.

What time did the neighbor get home? She flipped back through the paperwork until she came to the woman's interview. She had picked up her daughter from band practice and arrived home at approximately 7:30.

If someone framed Weaver, he or she could've killed Larson between 7:00 and 7:30.

Bliss rubbed her chin and stared at the wall as she considered this. The neighbor across the street didn't get home until after the police had entered, so it was possible.

Bliss turned back to Hale's report. The Texas Rangers were called in as soon as authorities realized a police officer had been killed. According to the report, Hale and Zane arrived at the scene at 9:22 p.m. the same night.

That wasn't surprising since sometimes it took rural law departments time to make the decision to call in other agencies. She set Hale's report aside and found Officer Montoya's report from the Liberty Police. His notes were not as detailed, but she skimmed the documents of the crime scene to check for inconsistencies. None jumped out. Her vision blurred, and she took another sip from her mug.

"Find anything useful?"

She jumped at the sound of Zane's voice, nearly spilling her coffee. "Don't scare me like that."

Amusement danced in his eyes. He stepped to her desk. "Did Hale make any mistakes?"

"Not that I could find. He was meticulous. But…"

"But…" Zane's eyebrows rose in anticipation.

"There was time for another shooter to be in the house. The neighbor only heard two shots, but there were three bullets. Someone else could've fired on Officer Larson between seven and seven thirty when he came through the door before Sean got home."

"The defense brought up the third bullet in the wall at the trial, and the prosecution argued since there were only two gun casings, the hole in the wall was made previously."

She shrugged. "Could be. Even if we could prove there was another shooter, we still don't have any strong suspects."

"Do you want to go get something to eat?"

She glanced up at his dark eyes. "I would love to, but I feel like I should keep working. Maybe if we could get the governor to give us a stay of execution…"

"It doesn't hurt to keep trying, but I don't see it happening. He was clear when Captain Brewer contacted him again earlier. The governor wants new evidence. He sarcastically said everyone on death row is innocent."

She leaned back in her chair. "What are you going to do?"

"Return to the center and keep checking out the tips. Someone must have seen something. Unless Lawrence took Wyatt to another state."

"I pray that's not true. If Lawrence's real desire is to save his brother, then I'd think he'd remain in Texas. If we could just find your grandson, we could put all of our efforts into figuring if Sean was framed." The pressure to locate Wyatt overwhelmed her. All she could picture was the last time she'd seen her son. Mitchell getting out of the vehicle and telling her bye—the image permanently planted in her mind.

Was Wyatt's mom going through the same thing? Sage had tried to stop his abduction. Were the if-only scenarios ruling her thoughts? If she'd held Wyatt's hand a little tighter in the parking lot. If she'd paid better attention to her surroundings. If she'd picked a different day to go shopping.

"In your experience, what should we be doing?" asked Zane.

Her experience hadn't saved her own child. She couldn't stop the thought from surfacing. "We follow every lead and keep digging into Lawrence's past to figure out where he took your grandson. Honestly, this makes only the third missing child case I've worked in which the child was held for ransom. Most are abducted by family members. Some run away. Few children are stolen by strangers, but those are taken for a variety of reasons. No two cases are the same. Sometimes we never know the reason the child was kidnapped."

His brown eyes searched her face.

She glanced away. Zane had always been good at reading her.

"I would've been there for you if you'd asked. I wish we would've never parted on bad terms, but I could've helped."

"You were married to Vivian. Besides, I handle my own problems." *You're a fraud*, she scolded herself. She'd always shied away from help. The truth was, she hadn't failed and shouldn't have been afraid to ask others for support. Right?

He didn't respond and she couldn't take the silence. "Since we haven't learned where he took Wyatt, the biggest asset we have is we know who has him. We keep probing into Lawrence's background to learn the most likely places he'd take him."

Zane nodded. "Most criminals go with what they're most familiar."

"Exactly. Lawrence grew up and attended school in a community ten miles from his current residence. He worked at the same location. We keep digging."

"Are you certain you don't want me to bring you something to eat?"

"I'm sure." She rubbed her forehead. "I'm going to delve deeper to see if we've overlooked anything pertinent. Give me another hour."

"You're exhausted."

She squinted. "I can rest later. I know my limits. But there's got to be something we're missing."

He put his hands up in a defensive motion. "Okay. I don't want you pushing yourself too hard. I'll holler if I learn anything."

She knew when to take a break. Working now could mean the difference between bringing Wyatt home and never seeing him again. She couldn't deal with the latter. Not again.

A few minutes after he left, Josie returned. "I'm going to visit with Montoya."

"One of the first officers on the scene?" At Josie's nod, she continued. "Anything I should know about?"

"No. I want to find out about the other officers' actions in the department at that time that might not have been in the report. Guerra moved to San Antonio twelve years ago, and he was kind enough to talk with me on the phone. He was at a birthday party for his kid and sounded distracted. I may try again at a later time."

"Thanks, Josie."

Two hours later, Bliss's eyes drifted shut, and she couldn't concentrate any longer. Even though it was only five thirty in the afternoon, she called Zane. As much as she wanted to keep working, she simply needed to get some sleep.

He came and picked her up. Even though she told

him she wasn't hungry, he pulled into a convenient store on the way to her house.

After a few minutes, Zane came back out of the store with a bag in his hand and strode across the parking lot. When he opened the door, the aroma of a mixture of grease and chocolate hit her.

"What in the world did you buy?"

He held out the large bag and slid a couple of drinks into the cup holder. "I didn't know what you were hungry for, so I bought a variety."

She peeked into the brown sack. Two chocolate cream-filled doughnuts, a PowerBar and another small brown bag. She didn't have to open it to know that it contained burgers and fries. She shook her head and smiled. "You must think I'm real hungry."

He shrugged and smiled. "I remember when we were younger, you could put away a large meal. You look like you're in great shape, so I wasn't certain if you were on a health kick."

Aww. That was sweet. But he didn't need to know how much that meant. Nowadays, it seemed if she looked at food, her pants fit too tight. "You don't look so bad yourself."

He busted out laughing and patted his stomach. "You've got to be joking."

She smiled in return but didn't comment on how good he looked to her. It must be an age thing. The tinge of gray in his hair and the tough, experienced look he portrayed would earn a double take even if she didn't know him.

"Are you going to make a choice so we can get back on the road?"

"Oh, sorry. The burger and fries smell delicious, but

I'll stick to the PowerBar and a bottle of water. I want to be on my game and not need a nap from the carb high."

"I don't have such qualms." He handed her the Power-Bar and dug out his burger. He put the truck into gear and pulled out of the parking lot while holding his food.

After they'd eaten, he dropped her off at the community center to get her Tahoe and followed her to her house. When they arrived, she quickly changed into fresh clothes. When she came back out, she stopped in her tracks.

The Texas Ranger's cowboy hat covered his eyes, and he was lying back in the recliner with his arms folded and one of his boots crossed over the other one.

She took in the sight and her chest ached. He was probably the most handsome man she'd ever known. Adam had been a nice-looking guy, too, but more in a clean-cut, let-me-get-the-door-for-you-and-help-you-in-the-kitchen sort. Comfortable. Not that there was anything wrong with that. He'd been attractive, too, and she'd been blessed to have him as a husband.

But Zane. Hmm. Zane was the no-nonsense, smoke-a-brisket-but-leave-me-out-of-the-kitchen type. He was a gentleman through and through, but also wouldn't back down from a fight if it needed fighting. He could send her blood pressure rocketing and the next minute make her feel better than anybody had a right to.

Uncomfortable.

He'd proposed the week of their one-year anniversary of dating. He'd taken her horseback riding on the trails behind his ranch. It had been a perfect day until they got into a fight over something so petty she couldn't remember what, but she was irritated. He'd chuckled and pulled her into his arms and stared into her eyes. "Marry me, Bliss."

She had said yes right then, which was unlike her to agree to anything quickly. But she'd been attracted to him since day one. Assuming he was used to getting his way, she'd played hard to get. It worked. Bliss had never been into lovers' games, but she'd realized Zane was different.

He was the first guy she'd truly wanted to be with. Maybe that was the reason she was happy to receive the offer to move to Atlanta—to know if what they had was real and if he'd come after her. He hadn't, but she hadn't answered his calls, either.

"Whatcha doing?"

"Oh, I thought you'd dozed off."

He climbed to his feet. "What has you so jumpy?"

"Nothing." She rolled her eyes, hoping he couldn't read her expression. "I won't sleep long, so I'll be out soon."

Zane looked at her. "Get all the rest you can. I'm going over the files now. I feel like we're missing something."

"Yeah, me too. I'm praying if we are, that we'll figure it out soon."

"Bliss, I appreciate all the work you're doing to bring Wyatt home."

"Thanks." She started to walk away but stopped and turned back. "I really appreciate you saying you would've been there for me. I was too stubborn to seek help back then." From Zane or her mom. If she'd told him about the loss of the baby, he would've come for her. She knew him well enough to know that much was true.

"Being independent can be a lonely life."

It was as if he read her thoughts. She shot him a smile and headed to her room. After brushing her teeth, she lay on her bed. The past and what-ifs kept crossing her mind. But she couldn't go back and hit the rewind button.

It was nice to have Zane here looking after her. She could hear his voice and figured he was talking on the phone. He was giving it all he had, but she was worried another day had gone by without any more sightings of Wyatt. When Mitchell had first disappeared, she'd gone three days without sleep. She kept praying the search would pay off if she was earnest enough.

Deal Lord, please be with Wyatt, wherever he is. Keep him safe. Amen.

As her eyes closed, she couldn't help but feel like the past was doomed to repeat itself. But if she couldn't be honest about her past, how would the future be better?

After Bliss went to lie down, Zane made a few more calls and then put on a pot of coffee. For the next hour, he pored over his notes on the Weaver case before settling back on the couch. At his own place, he was spoiled by having an oversize leather recliner. Anything smaller felt cramped, like he was sitting on children's furniture.

Bliss's words kept returning to him about needing to find where Lawrence might have taken his grandson. O'Neill had pulled up a detailed map near Lawrence's home. Two rangers and three Liberty police officers had driven by every business and residence for a fifteen-mile radius, checking all buildings or homes that were for sale or vacant.

So far, they had come up empty.

What were they missing? Where had Lawrence taken his grandson?

If Zane had kidnapped a child, he'd hunker down someplace out of the way and not leave. But Lawrence had tried that with the houseboat and was found. What if he didn't have a backup plan? Was he on the road? In a hotel in a nearby town? Had he ditched Wyatt and made a run for it? There was no way to know.

He pulled out the list of Liberty police officers who'd been with the department during the Weaver case: Montoya, Cunningham, Richards and Carpenter. Zane only remembered Montoya because he seemed to take the lead. Even though Jason became chief, he didn't remember him or Richards. He'd set up a time tomorrow to interview all four.

The chief of police at the time of the case was Sam Olson, since retired and in a rehab facility for a hip replacement.

Chasity ran a basic check on the officers, and no one stood out as a potential suspect. It was only eight thirty, so he called Dryden back and asked him to set up interviews with all four people who were in the department at the time of the Weaver case at seven in the morning.

A door opened, and Bliss padded out of her room. "I can't sleep. I need to talk to you."

Zane got to his feet and noted her ashen complexion. "Come on over. What's wrong?"

"There's been something I should've told you a long time ago." She stared him straight in the face, and a bad feeling washed over him.

"Hey, sit down. It can't be that bad." He followed her to the couch and sat close beside her. Even though she had broken off their engagement when they were younger, that was years ago. He was glad she was helping search for Wyatt. "We're a team. You can tell me anything."

Her brown eyes stared at the rug, and she squirmed in her seat. "I should've told you this a long time ago."

He smiled, trying to make her relax. "There's nothing you can't tell me."

A frown flattened her lips. "Zane…"

His hand cupped her chin and lifted where she had no choice but to look at him. "Just tell me. I'm not going to be mad."

"Yes, you are."

It wasn't like her not to speak her mind. He leaned closer and took her hand in his. "Get it over with and tell me."

"Right after I moved to Atlanta, we'd been fighting. I was excited about my job opportunity, but you didn't want me to move or postpone our wedding. My mom didn't want me to go off by myself, either. Of course, me and my mom's relationship had been rocky for a while."

"You're stalling." He said it playfully.

"I miscarried."

What? His mind tried to process the information. "You were pregnant? With *our* child?"

She nodded.

He released her hand and pulled back a little. "Is this why you left? You didn't want me to know you were going to have a baby?"

She shook her head. "No, it wasn't like that."

He got to his feet and looked up at the ceiling as questions swirled. He drew a breath. "Was I the father?"

"What?" Her voice grew louder. "Of course. There was no one else."

Out of all the things he could imagine she had to tell him, this was not on the list.

"I had quit going to church back then, but I wasn't promiscuous."

"Why?" He turned back to her. "Why didn't you tell me?"

She stood, and her leg gave way, almost making her fall before she caught her balance. "I wanted to. I didn't even realize I was expecting until after I moved into my apartment. I kept getting sick and chalked it up to the stress of our breakup and the nervousness of starting a new job far away from anyone I knew. And then I noticed the nauseous feelings only came in the mornings. I took a home test and it was positive. I made an appointment with a doctor. Before my first visit, I miscarried."

He stared at her. How could she keep it from him? Did she care so little for him that she didn't think it was important he knew?

His gut tightened. "If I had known, I would've flown to Atlanta to see you. Is this why you ignored my phone calls?"

She frowned. "I didn't want you to try to convince me to move back. Not then. After I lost the pregnancy, there was nothing you could do to change it."

He cocked his head at her. "I could've been there to help you grieve. Offer my support. You don't have to do everything alone, Bliss."

"I know." Her answer came out curt.

He ran his fingers through his hair, trying not to let her secret bother him. But it did. "I have interviews to do in the morning. I need to get ready. Will you be all right here by yourself?"

"You're free to go."

They stared at one another for a few awkward seconds. *You're free to go.* Those were the words he'd said to her when she broke off their engagement. "Lock up when I'm gone."

As he walked to his truck, he felt her watching him. He shut the door and glanced toward the house. He'd always had a soft spot for the former marshal, even after all this time. But when he opened his heart, it made him vulnerable—something he couldn't deal with. He needed to find his grandson and then return to normal. Even as the thought came, it brought him no peace to have Bliss out of his life.

ELEVEN

After Zane walked out, Bliss stared at the front door, waiting to see if he would come back in. Then, as his truck rumbled up the driveway, she turned off the lights and watched him disappear over the horizon.

This was why she hadn't told him. She'd hurt him. She'd seen it in his eyes and the way his jaw tightened, just like the night she returned his ring.

But she'd felt guilty for years for not telling him. Stuck in her cold apartment, she'd grieved alone. She never told anyone, not her mom and not Zane.

Zane and she had been young. She'd been stubborn. And he was right. It didn't hurt to reach out to others, but she wouldn't take advice. Months after the miscarriage, she finally started going back to church. Tried to get her thoughts on the straight path.

She prayed Zane would forgive her. She'd dealt with the grief years ago, but he'd just taken the blow. It would take time.

Bliss locked her house up tight and slid off her shoes. Her thigh continued to throb, so she took half of a pain pill. She changed into her sleeping shorts and oversize T-shirt, set her alarm clock for 8:00 a.m., plugged in her cell phone and put it on the nightstand.

With the gun in her grip, she climbed into bed and threw the covers over her head while leaving a small gap for air. She couldn't stand the feeling of not being able to breathe. Not claustrophobic, but maybe a little. She shoved the weapon inches from her hand for easy access and closed her eyes.

Mitchell's voice telling her bye seeped into her consciousness. He grabbed his superhero backpack from the floorboard, and a day-care teacher opened the door for him. Bliss glanced over her shoulder. "Daddy will pick you up from school today."

"Okay. Bye, Mama." Mitchell slammed the door and ran to the sidewalk. A drawing he'd colored for his teacher fell on the ground, and Bliss waited for him to scoop it up before she pulled away from the curb.

Bye, Mama. His words echoed in her mind again before being drowned out by a clanging.

The loud noise had her grabbing her gun and sitting up straight. Sweat beaded in her hairline. The sun shone brightly through the windows. What time was it? Had she overslept?

She looked at the clock. 7:47. Her alarm wasn't due to go off for thirteen minutes. She listened but only heard the central air running. She crept across the carpet and glanced out of her bedroom, listening intently. There was no movement or sound.

Mitchell telling her bye continued to play through her mind. Maybe she'd imagined the noise or had been dreaming about her son slamming the car door. But it had sounded so real. She wasn't taking any chances. She grabbed her phone and stepped out of her room.

A look at the front door revealed it was closed. She went into the kitchen and found the back door locked tight. Her shoulders slumped, the tension slowly sub-siding. The uneasy feeling still made her anxious, so she did a complete walk-through of the house. When that produced nothing that could've made the clanging noise, she slipped on her boots and stepped outside. A check of the garage showed her vehicle sitting outside where she had parked it.

Her home sat on three acres. Enough land to give her space between her neighbors, but also not so much that it was hard to maintain. She glanced across her place and spotted her elderly neighbor, Marjorie Henson, weeding her flower garden. As Bliss trekked around her backyard, birds flew from limb to limb, not seem-ingly alarmed.

She walked the perimeter of her home, not seeing anything off-kilter. Woods surrounded the east bor-der, and two squirrels chased each other. She lowered the gun to her side, and she wondered if the noise had been her ice machine. It sometimes could be loud, and this case had put her senses on high alert.

She stepped into her garage, and a moving shadow caused her to flinch.

As she started to spin around, someone grabbed her from behind and shoved a pillowcase over her head.

"You're gonna get that boy killed if you don't stop investigating. He'll be dead, just like Mitchell." The strong arm dug deep into her throat, choking the breath from her. Light filtered through the cloth, but she could only make out shapes. "Yeah, I know all about your son. If you would've moved faster, you could've saved him."

How was he familiar with Mitchell? Did he have knowledge about what happened after her son was abducted, or was he guessing? His arm pinned her right bicep, which held her gun. She gripped it tighter, so she didn't drop it. "What do you want?"

"Drop this case unless you want the boy's corpse sent to you in a body bag."

"I will. If you'll tell me where he's being hidden. I promise." That didn't mean Zane and the Texas Rangers would quit investigating. Lights floated before her eyes and wooziness threatened to overtake her. "Where is he?"

"Think about it. Where do you believe Mitchell was kept?"

As soon as his words were out, she was shoved hard against the back of her vehicle. Without taking seconds to remove the pillowcase, she spun and fired at the retreating figure.

She ripped the case off her head and chucked it to the ground. The intruder was gone. She ran to the side of the garage in time to see a man in black disappear into the woods.

At a sprint, she dashed after him. He couldn't get away.

A gunshot went off, making her flinch, but she didn't stop the pursuit. She made it to the protection of the trees and looked around. Another blast, and then he ran through the thicket. She took off and was running fast when a thick vine with thorns stabbed her leg.

Pain pulsed through her, and she tried to keep moving but only accomplished ten yards before she heard an engine. As she pushed her way through the brush, moisture spread over her thigh. The rumble faded away.

She hobbled toward the house as red emerged under her bandage, and she grabbed her cell phone and hit Zane's number.

"What's going on?"

"Our man was just here."

"At your house?"

"Yeah. He warned me away from the case. Said Wyatt would wind up dead, like Mitchell, if I didn't back off." She gathered some fresh bandages from her medicine cabinet and set her phone to speaker. Sagging into a dining chair, she started changing the dressings.

"Did you get a look at the guy or recognize his face?"

"No." She pulled off the old bandage, cringing. The wound was oozing blood, but not much. Most of the current bleeding came from where the thorn stabbed her. She'd have to be more careful. "He shoved a pillowcase over my head. I could only make out his silhouette."

There were a few seconds of silence. "What color was the pillowcase?"

"I didn't pay attention, but it's still in my garage. Hold on and I'll look." She got up and limped into her garage. She didn't mention her leg for fear it would worry Zane. Red droplets splattered the concrete. That wasn't her blood. She worked her way around the path where the shooter had escaped and found a couple more drops. "I may have hit him."

"As in, shot him?"

"Yeah." She quickly explained about firing in his direction as he took off.

"That's something. We'll keep an eye on the hospitals."

He'd moved fast, so she didn't think the injury was serious, but one never knew. In the garage, she scooped up the cloth. "Here's the pillowcase. It's white with lilac flowers. Is that the same as the kidnapper used on you?"

"No, mine was some sort of burlap bag that you might find at a craft store."

She considered that. "Do you think he was trying to make us believe it was the same guy?"

"Could be. I'm coming over."

"There's no need. I'm fine, and he's gone."

"I shouldn't have left last night."

She was quick to answer. "That's fine. What were you working on?"

"We're conducting interviews with all the members of the Liberty Police Department that were here sixteen years ago."

"How many are still here?"

"Four. That's not bad, considering it's such a small department. Jason—the chief, Montoya, Richards and Carpenter."

"Please stay and finish the interviews. I'll be fine."

"Are you certain?"

"Yes, please. We need to learn everything we can."

"Okay. Let me know if you need anything."

After they disconnected, she walked back into the house and applied a new bandage on her wound. The attacker's words kept returning to her about her son. Did he know how Mitchell had died? Like firsthand knowledge?

Adam's and Mitchell's killer had never been caught. Maybe if they'd discovered Mitchell sooner, but that hadn't happened. It had been almost three months since her boy had been found in that ditch and forensics suggested he'd been killed almost immediately. The cause of death was strangulation. Why had someone taken him? To sell on the black market? To abuse him somehow?

Maybe his abductor had taken him to get back at

her for a case she'd worked, just like Wyatt had been kidnapped as leverage against Zane. Investigators determined by the skid marks and broken glass on the side of the highway that the other vehicle had crashed into Adam's Altima head-on. Her husband had swerved and slammed on the brakes in an evasive maneuver, but the front end was damaged. The estimated speed of the other car was sixty on impact, and there was no evidence the other vehicle had hit their brakes. Maybe the wreck had been an accident, and the person had panicked. Intoxicated driver?

The scenarios were endless and succeeded in only giving her a headache. Now that she knew Mitchell wasn't alive and waiting to be rescued, it made her wonder if there was even a reason to keep trying to find the attacker. Like it was time to move on.

Her mind jumped back to Wyatt. What would happen after she helped rescue the lieutenant's grandson? If she could help locate this child, maybe her career could end on a positive note, and she wouldn't feel like her life had been for naught.

TWELVE

Zane entered the small room at the center that was set up with two tables and a few chairs. It was frustrating that these interviews were taking much longer than planned, because Montoya was late.

Jax O'Neill sat across from Jason Cunningham and should be about finished. Richards and Carpenter had already completed their interview, but they appeared clean, according to Jax. Zane doubted they'd learned anything more from the chief. So far, the men had answered all the questions, but nothing that led to new evidence. All they lacked was Montoya. He was the only one who still wasn't here, but Dryden was checking on him.

Being that it was Thursday, they were running out of time. Zane's mood had only grown worse with the case, and Bliss's conversation last night hadn't helped matters.

"Is there anything else I can help you with?" Jason looked from Jax to him.

Jax shook his head and then looked up at Zane. "What about you?"

Bliss going through the documents came to mind, and her question about the other bullet in the officer's report. Suddenly it came to him. "What about the third bullet?"

The chief coolly met his gaze. "What bullet?"

Jax watched Zane, but he didn't say a word.

"There were only two," Jason said.

Zane shook his head and dropped Montoya's report on the table. "There were three."

The chief picked up the papers and sifted through them. "Oh. I'd almost forgotten about that. I remember now. Investigators found the hole, but evidently it was put there at an earlier date. There were only two casings at the scene." He shoved the report back at Zane.

"How did Montoya know about it before it was found by the Rangers?" As both men stared at him, he put his finger on one of the papers. "Right there. Montoya wrote it down before the hole was discovered by investigators. Was there a third casing at the scene?"

Jason shook his head. "You'll have to ask him."

"I'll do it."

"If you are through with me…" He pushed back from his chair and stood. "I'm sorry I couldn't be of more help."

"I appreciate it." Zane held out his hand, and the chief took it.

After Cunningham left the room, Jax asked, "What was that about?"

"Just a feeling. I believe Sean was framed. If he was, someone has to know something. It's the only thing that is different in the reports."

"How did Montoya know about the other bullet?"

Zane's cell phone buzzed, and Dryden's number came across the screen. He smiled. "We're about to find out." He hit Accept. "Where's our man?"

"Dead."

"Wait." The air was knocked from him, and he had to take a deep breath. "What happened?"

"I just went by the police department, since he was coming off his shift. He was sitting in his cruiser, parked out back away from camera range. A self-inflicted gunshot wound to the head."

"Did you hear that?"

Jax nodded.

"If Montoya was the one to frame Sean, then we need to find evidence quick to save a man from execution. I'm going to find my grandson."

After Zane walked out of the room, Sage came through the front door and made a beeline toward him.

He drew a deep breath.

"What's going on?"

"We're still investigating. We have a few leads."

Her green eyes scrutinized him. "It doesn't look good. Does it?"

As much as he wanted to lie, he couldn't. Wouldn't. False hope was cruel. "No, honey, we don't know where he's at, but know we're doing everything in our power to bring Wyatt home. I can promise you that. Continue to pray."

"Oh, Daddy." Tears sprang to her eyes. She took a step back. "I need my son. I want you to find him."

"Can I ask you something?" He'd been walking on eggshells around her, but he was curious. "Where is Wyatt's daddy?"

Her face fell, and she glanced away. "We're separated at the moment. But we're working on it."

He waited for more explanation, but none came.

"Okay. If you need to talk with someone, there's a lady who volunteers with Bliss who can help you."

"I just need my son home, and everything else will work out." She frowned. "You own this."

"I will find him."

She turned around and left him standing there.

His jaw tightened. How could everything go so wrong? He glanced over, and the chief was watching him.

Irritation flew all over him, and he walked out. As he went to get in his truck, Jax O'Neill hollered at him. "Lieutenant."

"Yeah. This better be good news."

Jax jogged over. "We received a call from a lady who thought she saw a man with a child with Wyatt's description. Dryden is on his way to visit her. You want to go?"

"Yes. Let me swing by and pick up Bliss."

He called her as soon as he was in his truck. He explained about the tip. "Would you like to go with me?"

"You know I do."

At least if Bliss was mad at him for how he reacted to the news of her miscarriage, it didn't stop her from staying on the case. A few minutes later, he pulled up to her house. Instead of waiting for him to come to the door, she hurried up the sidewalk and climbed into his truck.

She stared out her window.

"I'm sorry," Zane said.

"You have nothing to apologize about."

He looked at her. "I should've been there for you."

"You didn't know."

She always had to have the last word. He almost

laughed. But if he'd gone after her like he should have, he would've been there. It'd be best to keep that thought to himself. He seemed to hurt those he loved the most.

The thought of Sage being out of his life really struck home. The more he reflected on it, the more it disturbed him. Sage and her husband were separated. What did they do for a living? Did they live in town or in the country? Was Sage able to stay at home with Wyatt, or did she work? Did her husband's parents fill the role of grandparents?

He knew nothing of the adult she'd become. One thing was certain: he intended to try again to mend their relationship. Even if he had to quit being a Texas Ranger.

A knot formed in his stomach at the thought.

He'd turned forty-five this past April and couldn't fathom retirement or starting a new career at this point in his life. He'd never wanted to do anything else except be in law enforcement. Most people either ate, drank and bled being an officer or ran faster than a Stetson in a hurricane.

But Bliss had already said she planned to quit the Bring the Children Home Project. He glanced her way.

"What?" Her eyebrows shot up.

He shrugged. "After this case, what are you going to do?"

"Concerning what?" She rubbed her thigh. "I guess you mean besides heal."

"You mentioned you planned to turn your organization over to Riggs and Annie Brenner. Their reputation precedes them." He noted she became very still. "Are you considering going back to the marshals?"

"No." She shook her head. "I haven't decided. I just know what I *don't* want to do."

Zane gave her another look. "You don't sound pleased with your choice."

"Nothing makes me happy nowadays. Not trying to be cynical, but all I know is I can't keep looking for children. There's got to be more."

Since she couldn't bring her own child home. Her unspoken words shouted volumes, and he wondered how he would feel if he couldn't save Wyatt. Probably the same way.

The rest of the drive to the caller's residence, his mind returned to the case at hand and prayed that the lady who thought she'd spotted Lawrence and Wyatt gave them a good lead. Not like the last one.

The quaint house sat nestled on the edge of town on a dead-end street. Flower beds bloomed in vibrant colors due to the recent rains, and the lawn was bright green for Texas. Dryden's truck was parked in the drive behind a white sedan.

"Hopefully, we'll learn something helpful." Bliss climbed out of his vehicle.

"My thoughts exactly." A Welcome sign leaned against the side of the house. He rapped on the door, and a woman's voice hollered that it was open and to come in.

He held it ajar for Bliss and then stepped inside. Cool air hit him, and the smell of corn bread filled the air. A woman with graying hair sat at the kitchen table with Dryden.

The ranger introduced them. "This is Velma Ray. And this is Lieutenant Adcock and Bliss Walker."

"Have a seat," she offered. They hadn't even taken

their chairs before she started in. "I saw that man and child you're looking for."

When a story broke on the news, many times, they received a lot of calls that led to nowhere. Well-meaning people could hope to assist and make mistakes. But that wasn't always so. "Can you describe what they looked like and the location?"

"Certainly. I've been telling Ranger Dryden here all about it. I'd just left the Piggly Wiggly on the east side of town when this older-model black Chevy pickup flies up on my bumper and almost hits me. He blew his horn and then whipped around me. As always, it doesn't do you no good round here to speed, because the red light's gonna catch you. I pulled up beside him to give him a dirty look, and that's when I noticed the little boy crying in the passenger seat."

This could be promising.

Bliss asked, "Did you notice what either of them was wearing?"

"Sure did. The boy had on a red shirt, and his hair was all messed up, like he forgot to comb it after getting out of the bath. When the man saw me looking, he pushed the boy down into the seat. He was in such a hurry he didn't wait for the light to turn green but took off after the traffic cleared. I had been watching the news when I realized I was out of butter. My Warren had his heart set on sausage, beans and corn bread. Bread just ain't the same without butter."

The aroma of homemade cooking had Zane's stomach growling. Beans and corn bread had been a childhood favorite of his grandma's that he didn't appreciate until he was an adult. He smiled, prodding Velma to continue. "Did you notice which way he went?"

"Notice?" She laughed. "I followed him. I knew it must be the kidnapper. Looked just like the boy on the news."

Zane and Bliss exchanged looks. That was a dangerous move, but he appreciated the woman's spunk.

Velma leaned forward on her elbows. "I followed him several miles east of town, but I kept my distance, like they do in the TV shows and movies. I didn't want to spook him and take the chance he'd hurt the boy. When he got to Ellis Cemetery Road, he took off fast and left me in the dust. I had to back off and lost him."

"When was this?"

"About three hours ago. I called the tip line as soon as I arrived home, but it took a while for anyone to return my call."

"I understand. We're slow sometimes." That was only half-true. Mostly, there were a lot of tips to sift through when the news first came out. "Is there anything else you think might be important?"

"No, sir. I hope you find that child. I called my sister, and she said the boy is the grandson of one of your rangers."

"Yes, ma'am." The news had not shared that bit of information, but it only took one person to repeat details for the word to get out. He glanced at Bliss. "Do you have any questions?"

She shook her head but held a business card out to Velma. "We appreciate your help. If you think of anything else, could you give me a call?"

"Would be glad to. I hope you find the boy."

Bliss said, "Thanks."

Once they were in the truck, Zane drove quickly out of the neighborhood. The sun hung low in the sky. They didn't have much time before it became dark, and he'd hoped to make it to Ellis Cemetery Road before then. No matter what, he wanted a thorough search, even if conditions weren't perfect.

They were both quiet as he ate up the highway. Miles outside of town, he almost missed the turn to the country road. He hit his brakes and backed up. Then he took off again. Potholes cluttered the surface, so he kept his speed down to forty.

"Keep your eyes open." At her look, he laughed. "I get it. You know your job."

She smiled. "I hope this is not another dead end. Lawrence could've noticed Velma following him and simply turned down this road to get her off his trail. As far as we know, he could be almost in Arkansas by now."

Bliss was right. Lawrence wasn't stupid. All in all, he didn't think the man was violent, but if he had nothing to lose, you never knew how desperate he'd become. "I pray that's not so."

"Me too."

The road curved and wound around through the countryside. They passed a couple of farmhouses, but mostly open pastures, with a spattering of trees and herds of cattle. The path came to a Y, which forced him to slow down. Darkness fell fast and his headlights automatically came on. No road signs existed, but the well-traveled route was to his right. He took it. After another quarter of a mile, the cemetery appeared on his left, complete with an open iron gate. Above the entrance was a sign indicating the cemetery was founded in 1852. He planned to cruise on by when Bliss pointed.

"There's a pickup."

Zane hit his brakes. Sure enough, under the protection of a giant pecan tree sat a truck. He pulled into the drive. Tall monuments towered in the shadows, but his headlights reflected off the brake lights. A pit formed in his stomach as he approached. "Do you see anyone?"

Bliss leaned forward. "No. But it's getting hard to see. There's no one inside the cab."

He didn't locate anyone, either, but that didn't mean Lawrence wasn't hunkered down in the seat. Zane retrieved his gun from his holster and grabbed his flashlight from the console. "Let me check out the truck."

"I'm going with you."

Taking in their surroundings, he walked behind the bed to her side with the flashlight off. He looked to make certain this wasn't an ambush, but there were literally hundreds of hiding places. He whispered, "Stay out of the light."

Keeping to the left, they moved beside a tree and then to another. All the while, both of them had their guns ready. He kept his ears trained for the sound of movement or the voice of a child. Besides a slight breeze, the only noise was that of crickets and a frog from somewhere nearby.

She approached the passenger side while he moved to the driver's. Something felt off. It was too quiet. Maybe Lawrence ditched this truck but had another vehicle waiting. That was a good possibility.

He stepped to the truck and peeked through the window. "Clear."

They opened the doors, and the interior light came on. A piece of half-eaten taffy sat on the passenger seat. Bliss said, "I think Wyatt was in here."

"Looks like you're right. Unless Lawrence and Wyatt

were never in the truck because it belongs to someone else." He shone his flashlight on the surrounding ground. Deep ruts were left in the grass from truck tires. No other tracks were nearby.

She came around the front of the vehicle and examined the land. "Doesn't appear that he had another mode of transportation stashed at the cemetery."

"I was thinking the same thing."

"Shine it on the ground right there." She pointed beneath the driver's door. "Maybe the rain soaked in, but I'd think Lawrence would leave footprints."

With his light on the grass, he continued around the truck to the passenger side. "There's one set of prints headed toward the trees."

"Only the top half of the shoe, like he was running."

"Could be. With Velma following him, Lawrence could've hurried out of here while carrying Wyatt."

"That would make sense."

They persisted in scouting around the grounds, only occasionally spotting prints. When they came to the trees, another set of tire tracks—smaller than truck tires—emerged. And more indentations. Someone else was here. "More tracks."

"Those aren't the same as the person in the truck, and it looks like whatever vehicle they belonged to came and went."

As they neared the woods, his light reflected off something small and shiny. Before he completely walked up on it, he could tell it was a bullet casing.

A pile of dirt created a dark shadow. His heart constricted. *Please, don't be Wyatt.* Surely, Lawrence would not harm a little boy.

"Oh no." Bliss gasped. "Is that what I think it is?"

"It appears to be a fresh-dug grave." Had the man hurt his grandson? Zane didn't want to look but instead glanced heavenward. How would he tell Sage? And Bliss hadn't wanted to help him because she said she needed to escape this kind of life. What had he been thinking?

With a deep breath, he strode toward the hole and tried to prepare himself for the worst. Bliss, bless her heart, moved to his side.

Please, God, how do I protect her when everything is spinning out of control? I need help. Now.

THIRTEEN

Bile rose in Bliss's throat as she stared into the shallow grave at the back of the man's lifeless body. She swallowed the sour taste and eked out, "I suppose this is Lawrence."

Zane was quiet as he knelt by the mound of dirt. A large dark spot spread over the back of the guy's skull. Zane reached in and lifted the victim's chin, rolling his head slightly. "It's him."

She tried not to look, but like a bad car wreck, her gaze landed on the man's face. Her knees shook as she spun on her heel. Even though she'd worked with the marshals for years, she could never get used to seeing dead people. "I'll never understand how someone could shoot a person from behind. Nothing more cowardly." And then she said what had to be going through Zane's mind. "How will we find Wyatt now?"

"Wait…"

"For what?" Her body ached from tension, but at his hopeful tone, she held her breath.

He felt Lawrence's wrist. "He's still warm. Either he was hit a few minutes ago, or… I'm getting a weak pulse."

"How?" Victims shot in the head rarely survived.

She looked over Zane's shoulder into the uncovered grave. "We have to save him."

"The wound is seeping but not bleeding heavy, at least not anymore." Zane stood. "Let me call this in, and then we'll search to see if Wyatt is nearby."

She only halfway listened as the lieutenant called in their location to the Rangers and 9-1-1. Someone had intended to silence the kidnapper for good. Her gaze sought out signs of a child walking over the ground, but it was too dark.

Please, Lord, help the boy to safety. Lead us to him.

As she silently spoke with God, her brain continued thinking of the little boy she'd held days before. His sweetness and fear. She'd made a promise to take him to his mom. It was all he wanted.

Possible scenarios ran through her mind. Had Zane's grandson gotten away and was hiding nearby? If Lawrence wasn't planning on hurting his victim, maybe he told Wyatt to run. Or maybe the suspect grabbed the boy. Or whoever tried to execute Lawrence also hurt Wyatt. She wouldn't go there. Couldn't. No, he was alive. Had to be. They just needed to find him.

Zane moved beside her and shone the light on the ground. In silence, he eased around the perimeter, searching for signs of his grandson, but found nothing.

Finally, he said, "The Rangers and Chandler with his K-9 are on their way. Captain Brewer is trying to secure a helicopter with thermal imaging. If Wyatt is close, we'll find him."

"I pray it's so. What's going on?" She let out a deep, ragged breath. "Why would someone attempt to kill Lawrence?"

The dim moonlight provided enough light to see his

eyes. "Lawrence had to be right, and his brother was framed. The real killer doesn't want us to learn the truth."

"But how will that help? They know we'll keep looking."

His shoulders fell. "The person plans to get rid of us, too."

Boom! A gun blasted just as a bullet whizzed past her head.

"Take cover!" Zane yelled.

She couldn't tell which direction the shooter was, but it sounded like the woods behind them. Instead of lying on the ground, she hunkered low and ran for Zane's truck. She wasn't going to let some killer scare her away. She had no family. If she had to die to save that little boy, so be it.

Zane started to return fire into the thicket, but he'd be shooting blind. He couldn't take the risk of hitting his grandson.

Several more bullets zinged past her. Quickly, she opened the driver's door and slid into the seat. Keeping her head down, she turned the key and started the truck. She put it into gear while peeking over the steering wheel. The headlights reflected from the trees and off something shiny. Another vehicle?

Careful not to run over any gravestones, she eased forward until Zane fired two quick shots. He sprinted around the back of the truck, and he climbed into the passenger seat, slamming the door. "Do you see him?"

"I think there's a vehicle over there." She pointed to the woods and off to the right.

"I see it. Go."

"Okay. Hang on. It's muddy." She hit the gas and

kept between the rows of headstones. When she came to the edge of the cemetery, she wove her way in between the trees, but several appeared in front of her, blocking her path. She put the truck into Reverse. The tires spun and kicked up mud until they finally found traction and shot backward. This time, she followed a narrow trail through the woods.

"There he goes." Zane pointed. He rolled down his window. "Get me closer."

"Okay." She gained speed as she plowed over rocks and bushes. They bounced with each hit, but she couldn't see the man anymore.

"To your left. Left."

She jerked her wheel. "Be careful. We don't know where Wyatt is."

He didn't respond as he leaned out the door with one hand hanging on to the inside of the window frame and his right holding his gun. He took aim and fired again.

A large wash sat at the bottom of the trail. She didn't want to lose this guy. As she put her foot on the gas, she hollered, "Hang tight."

The truck tore down the embankment, the wash deeper than she'd expected. They hit with a jolt, the truck bouncing up and down. She kept the accelerator pressed to the floor, but the wheels sank and spun. Water flew behind them, but the tires dug lower.

"Stay here." Zane leaped out of the truck and took off through the woods.

"Be careful." The words faded into the night. She shifted into Park and stepped out of the tall truck. The mud came up to her ankles. As she trekked out of the wash, her feet struggled with each step and created a sucking noise. The muck clung to the sides, making it heavy and more difficult to move. *Great.* At least the mud hadn't seeped inside.

Suddenly, she stepped off into a hole, and water poured into her shoes. *Fantastic.*

Once she was on relatively dry ground, she sat and took off her shoes while keeping her gun safely beside her hand for quick access. Water spewed onto the ground. After she put her shoes back on, she stood and looked about to make sure the shooter hadn't circled back around. Mud caked the side of Zane's truck, and the tires were over half submerged. A wrecker would probably need to be called to get it out.

Somewhere in the distance, the roar of an engine broke through the nighttime sounds. She listened, trying to get the gist of where it originated. It could be law enforcement or the shooter. Suddenly, more engines sounded.

She turned about and headed back to the cemetery, following the path she'd created. Zane would know where she'd gone. As she stepped around a thick cedar tree and came out on the other side, something large moved.

"Careful." Quick as lightning, she pointed her weapon.

"Would you get the barrel of your gun out of my gut?" Zane said calmly.

She let out an awkward laugh. "You might want to warn me when traipsing through the woods while a gunman is on the loose."

"I could say the same for you." He pushed her gun away.

"Touché." They walked beside each other on the slick trail. "I'm assuming he got away."

"He did. Not certain, but I might have hit him."

"That could be promising if he seeks medical help." She tried not to let the implications sink in, but the case seemed to be falling apart. Wyatt had vanished, and his kidnapper was barely alive. Had she really agreed to this case just to have the whole thing crumble in her hands? She couldn't take another loss. Any good news was welcome. "Did you happen to see what vehicle he was driving?"

"No. But investigators can at least figure out what type by examining the tracks."

Time was ticking. Not only with Sean Weaver's execution, but if Wyatt was hidden somewhere, could they find him before he was injured or was lost for good?

Texas Rangers Dryden and O'Neill looked up as they walked into the cemetery. "I'm assuming this is our kidnapper."

Zane let out a breath. "I'm afraid so."

The weight of the situation took its toll. Not only was Bliss exhausted from lack of sleep and being shot in the leg, but emotionally, she was running out of steam.

Jax O'Neill was a tall, rugged cowboy type, and Luke Dryden had a friendly, welcoming manner. She liked Zane's team of rangers. But even being surrounded by professional lawmen, she felt like they were losing ground.

Chandler approached her and held out a foam cup. "Thought you could use some coffee."

"Thanks." She took it from him, even though she wasn't hungry or thirsty. Her shoulders were weighed down as if she were carrying an elephant.

Frustration bit at her. And something else crawled around her emotions—fear. Fear so terrifying, like she'd never felt before. After Mitchell went missing, she had confidence she'd find him, as though if she searched hard enough, long enough, they'd have a reunion. It kept her moving. Gave her hope.

But now? Now she had nothing but doubt and a feeling of loss. Every move brought her uncertainty. Running in the woods with killers, if she hesitated, could spell disaster for not only her but others.

While she and two other Liberty officers combed the area looking for signs of Wyatt, Zane visited the other officers by the vehicle presumably left by Lawrence. He stood tall and took command of the situation. He'd always been a leader. Even when they were dating, and he was a state trooper, he'd been a natural. The rangers who worked under him respected him.

The lieutenant trusted she could bring his grandson home. Had he made a mistake? The thought put excruciating pressure on her.

A few minutes later, he strode over to her. "Are you okay?"

"Fine."

"Bliss." He rested his hands on her shoulders. "How's the leg? Are you hurting? I know the trek through the woods couldn't have been easy on you."

She started to deny the constant throb in her thigh but decided against it. Zane was too good at reading people, and what purpose would it serve? "It hurts like fire, and I'm getting too old for stuff like this. But it's nothing I can't handle. I've had worse injuries."

The corner of his mouth quirked. "I'm there with you. Let me know if I need to take you home so you can get some rest."

She nodded. He dropped his hands, and instantly, she felt cooler after his warmth evaporated.

"We're going to continue searching and pulling our information together. So far, we've found no footprints or signs left by Wyatt. Is there anything else we should be doing?"

"You're asking me?" The simple gesture surprised her. Back in their younger days, he never would've asked.

He shrugged it off as if it were a common occurrence. "I am."

Satisfaction that he trusted her eased some of her uncertainty. Now, if she could only not let him down. "I'd love to keep checking the tips coming in. It's one thing that often is not put as a top priority, and there's always someone out there that has seen something. Just like Velma."

"A couple of Liberty PD's investigators are sifting through the calls. Josie and Chasity are still talking with Ike Harris's family."

Bliss needed to call Josie and see if there were any leads. If Harris had framed Sean for the murder of Officer Larson, it was going to be more time-consuming to prove. Not impossible but difficult. As she shifted her weight, pain shot down her leg, causing her to cringe. "Oh."

Zane cocked his head. "Go home and rest. Start fresh in the morning."

"After we get through at the community center, I'd rather go to the hospital and see if Lawrence wakes up. I can rest, but if he's awake even for a bit, I want to be there."

"That's a good idea. Let me get my truck unstuck, and I'll drop you off."

Did the suspect know Lawrence had survived the shooting? If so, that put Wyatt's abductor in grave danger, like her and Zane. Who would've thought she'd fight so hard to ensure a kidnapper lived?

Zane was glad the ride to the command center was in silence. "I want you to be careful."

In the darkness of the cab, Bliss looked at him. The glow of the dashboard lit up her features enough to see the question in her eyes. "I'm always cautious."

"I know you are. You were an excellent marshal and even better at finding missing children."

"But?"

How did he say she was important to him and that he didn't want to lose her without sending the wrong message? Even after Bliss left for Atlanta to train to be a marshal, he thought of her often. If he was honest, he'd admit occasionally he wondered how things would've turned out if he'd been patient when she wanted to delay their marriage. But he didn't like it when his mind went in that direction. Vivian had been a good wife whom he'd loved. Yes, she was different than Bliss, but their relationship had been uncomplicated and enjoyable. Then there was Sage, who'd made their life complete.

Bliss continued to stare at him, not willing to let him off the hook.

"As with my rangers, at the end of the day, I want everyone to go home to their families." By the glare she sent him, maybe that didn't come out right. "Listen. We're in this together."

"Yeah, I know." Her head bobbed. "Please don't coddle me. It hasn't been that long since I worked in law enforcement."

"I didn't say that."

"You don't have to. Is it because I'm a woman? I didn't think you were that kind of guy."

"That's not it." This conversation had taken a bad turn. "You know me. I've never believed women any less capable. While we concentrate on trying to find Wyatt, someone is attempting to kill us. Don't let your guard down. I care about you. There. Are you happy? I lost my wife. My daughter hasn't spoken to me in years. And I have a grandson I didn't know I had who's been kidnapped. I don't even know if he's still alive." The words rushed out before he had time to give them thought.

Her lips pressed into a thin line, and she turned toward the window.

Great. He'd probably come off as paranoid—something he didn't plan on doing. But he wouldn't take it back. The day Vivian died, she'd tried to call him three times, and each time, he replied that he would call her back. When Sage stormed out of the house, he didn't know what to say. Her attacks had made him defensive, and he didn't offer her what she desired—love and patience.

Zane wouldn't make the mistake again of not letting people he cared about know what he was thinking.

"I understand." Her face softened. "I'll be careful."

He glanced at her, and in that moment, an understanding passed between them. They were both in the same boat, having lost their families. Neither could afford to lose anyone else.

They rode the rest of the way in silence. He thought

about the case, planning his next moves, and he was certain Bliss was doing the same.

He walked her inside the building, and the first thing he saw was Sage lying on the couch. He crossed to her, and his heart melted. The overhead lights were turned off, but illumination from the hallway cast enough light to see. She lay with her head on an uncomfortable pillow and used a different one to cover her arms. A box of tissues sat on the floor, and one was wadded in her hand. No doubt she'd cried herself to sleep.

His boot made a slight scrape on the tile, and his daughter's eyes flitted open.

She sat. "Did you find him, Daddy?"

His chest tightened at the name *Daddy*, but he hated he didn't have better news. "Not yet. But we're still working on it."

"Oh." Her face went slack, and she turned her attention to Bliss. "What are y'all doing here, then?"

Bliss moved forward. "I came back here to go through the tip line. You're welcome to join me."

Confusion crossed his daughter's brow, but it morphed. "I'd like that."

"I'll be in the office." Bliss glanced at him. "I'll see you later."

"Okay. Let me know if you learn anything." He watched her walk with a slight limp down the hall to the room where the investigators had been working. He turned to Sage. He wanted to tell her to take it easy on Bliss, that she was hurting, but he held back. His daughter was experiencing a terrible trauma, too.

"Have you learned anything new?" Her words were noncombative.

How did he tell her that things were worse? He'd always talked straight, but knowing the truth would hurt his daughter. "We found the kidnapper—"

"That's great."

He moved his hands downward, telling her to hold on. "Not so fast. He's been shot, Sage."

"What do you mean?" She scowled. "What happened?"

"We followed a tip to the Ellis Cemetery on the outskirts of town. We discovered what we believed to be the kidnapper's truck, and Lawrence Weaver had been shot. He's alive—barely. He's being care-flighted to the local hospital. Wyatt was not there."

Despair filled her eyes, and her hands covered her mouth. "Where is my son? How are we going to find him now?"

"Sage…" He reached for her hand, but she jerked away.

"No, Dad. This is all your fault. Somebody used my son as leverage against you because you're a Texas Ranger. He's just a little boy."

"I know, baby. Uh, Sage. Sorry." What could he say but apologize? She was right. He never liked when others were blamed for a criminal's activities. He'd always argued with the reasoning. But for the first time in his life, he agreed. His grandson would be at home with his mama at this moment if it weren't for him.

Tears glistened in her eyes, and her head fell. "I'm sorry. I know you didn't mean for this to happen. Sometimes when I was a little girl, I'd wish you were a businessman or something. Some kind of job where you weren't in danger or had to miss my ball games."

A knife to the heart wouldn't have hurt more. He remained silent and let her vent her anger. He'd hoped when his daughter had gotten older, she would understand. Memories of her posing with him at the Texas Ranger Museum and her wearing a pink cowboy hat and a Junior Texas Ranger badge crossed his mind. That was back when she was still daddy's little girl. He had the urge to explain, but he held his tongue.

She sighed. "What can I do to help?"

"Pray Lawrence gets better so he can tell us where he hid Wyatt."

Disbelief traversed her features, and then she gave a solid nod. "Okay. I'll do it. But what if Lawrence doesn't have Wyatt, and the man who shot him does?"

"That thought has crossed my mind, too. Continue to pray. If an investigator asks you something, answer. We're moving as fast as we can."

Bliss stepped out of the office and stood in the hall, waiting for him. She motioned him over.

"Excuse me." He strode over to Bliss. "Have you learned anything?"

"Maybe." Her gaze flitted to Sage, and she lowered her voice. "Come with me."

He prayed she'd learned another good tip. Right now, he didn't think he could take bad news.

FOURTEEN

Bliss had a bad feeling about this caller, but she wanted to get Zane's take on it before coming to any conclusions. The look in his eyes just about did her in, but there was no time to check out things first before mentioning it. She held out her cell phone. "Look at this text. It just came in."

You are wasting your time. Sean Weaver murdered that cop. I was there and have proof. If you want to see the boy alive, be at the Shake and Cake in ten minutes. If you bring any of the police or Rangers with you, the boy is dead.

Zane's eyebrows furrowed. "You're not going alone."

The authority in his tone irked her, but there was no time for that. She held her hands in the air. "I told you about the message, didn't I?"

"This is a setup, Bliss. As far as we know, there are more explosives on my loaner truck. And how did this person get your number?"

"I don't know. I won't drive your truck. And I know chances are slim this guy really wants to help. But if this is the real killer of Officer Larson, we have to do something. It may be our only chance to find Wyatt. We don't have time to come up with a good plan. I'm going, and I'd like you to follow me. Besides, that place should be lit up."

His face turned red. "Okay. I'll take somebody's minivan, and hopefully the guy won't know it's me. When you get there, call me and keep me on the line. Let's go." ·

She stepped over to Josie Hunt and discreetly said, "I need the keys to your vehicle. Don't ask questions."

The investigator's brown eyes searched her face for answers, and then she quietly removed her keys from her pocket, handing them over.

Bliss padded down the hall and out the back door. Before she stepped out, she caught a glance of Sage watching her with a questioning eye. Zane had stopped at the door but would come out in a minute.

Bliss did a quick survey of the parking lot but only saw a young investigator leaning against the building holding a cigarette between his fingers and talking on his cell phone. She hurried around the building to Josie's Ford Bronco. After performing a hurried walk around to look for explosives and not seeing any, she climbed into the vehicle. Ten minutes didn't give her much time, so she moved fast. She shifted into Drive and took off.

As she kept an eye on her rearview mirror, she got her thoughts together about this meeting. *It's a setup.* Zane's words kept replaying through her mind, and she knew it was very possible. Maybe even likely. But she had no choice.

At least Zane hadn't insisted on going with her.

She slowed as she came to the intersection. A glance

to the minivan to her left caused her to do a double take. How had the lieutenant made it there before her? He must've taken a shorter route.

She turned into the dark parking lot of Shake and Cake on her right. The security lights were off, and no vehicles were around. Out of her peripheral vision, she saw the minivan pull onto the highway and slowly drive out of sight. Quickly, she called Zane. He picked up before the ring finished, and she slid her cell phone into her back pocket.

"I'm going in. Can you hear me?"

"I hear you fine."

With her gun in her hand, she exited the Bronco and glanced around. All was silent until a rattling of a truck pulling a cattle trailer approached on the highway. After it whizzed by, the silence grew. A June bug danced on the concrete slab and flew into the air. She stepped toward the building. "Hello. Anyone here?"

Sunflowers grew against the side of the block building and danced in the wind. Several blue fifty-five-gallon drums and an old clunky watercooler could be seen in the back of the store. With her gun ready, she walked toward the only place someone could hide behind—the barrels.

Lids were secured in place, and it made her wonder what the bakery would've used them for. The city would require trash service, so it wouldn't be that. She slowed as she approached the first barrel.

Raar. Something skittered out from between two drums, making Bliss jump.

"Stupid cat." She put her hand to her heart. After another glance around, her focus went back to the blue barrels. She remembered watching a true crime show where a serial killer had kept his victims inside drums like this. Now, why would someone leave a tip alerting them to something as heinous as that?

Still. She stepped to the first container. The wind blew her hair into her face, and she shoved it aside. The reflection of the minivan could no longer be seen. Did Zane leave?

She lifted the lid on the closest barrel and peered in. A dark, crusty substance.

Someone cleared his throat, causing her to jump.

She spun with her gun aimed. "Who's there?"

A man blended into the shadows behind the Shake and Cake. "Let's not worry about names."

Her heart pounded fast. She hadn't seen any vehicles. Had the man come on foot? "You said you had proof Sean Weaver killed Officer Larson."

"I lied about that, but I didn't want any police or Texas Rangers around."

This was not good. She gripped her gun and took a step to the left behind the watercooler. "What do you want?"

"Someone else shot that cop that night."

Was it possible they had their first witness? "How do you know?"

"I was in the house behind Weaver's home and across the creek. I heard a gunshot."

That street was nearly forty yards away. "How do you know it wasn't Sean Weaver?"

"Because his car wasn't home."

"What time was this?"

"About seven fifteen."

The timeline would fit. Slowly, she made her way farther into the shadows. She surveyed the area around the building but didn't see Zane. Where was he? "How

come you didn't come forward when Sean was arrested? You could've saved a man from death row."

"I was afraid. I was just a seventeen-year-old kid.
But it's always bothered me. I want y'all to catch the
real killer."

Bliss still wasn't certain she could trust this witness, but he sounded believable. "Did you see anyone
around Sean's house? Any strange cars?"

"Not on the street Sean lived on. But there was one
on Throckmorton. Parked in front of an abandoned
house."

This witness could break the case wide open, but
she needed him to make a formal statement. He hadn't
answered her other question. "This is a great help, but
I need more information."

"I can't do that. I have a wife and two kids. They
can't find out."

She drew a deep breath. "Did you see anyone?"

"Yes, but—"

Headlights crossed the parking lot and approached
from the side of the building. The vehicle was pulling
around back.

"You shouldn't have brought anyone with you!" The
guy darted along the side of the building and sprinted
for the tall grass just as a Liberty police car stopped
in the drive.

"Wait!" She hurried after him, but he disappeared
into the brush.

A young officer stepped out of his car and pulled
his gun. "Are you okay?"

The loud sound of a motorcycle rumbled and raced
away.

"Yeah." She held her finger in the air, telling him

to hold on as she pulled her cell phone out of her back pocket. "Did you see him?"

"Trying to catch him now."

"Okay." She turned back to the officer. "How did you know I was meeting someone?"

Instead of answering, the twentysomething lawman demanded, "What's going on here? That guy looked familiar."

"I received a tip, and the informer wanted no officers around. How did you know about my meeting?"

He shrugged. "Chief Cunningham asked me to check on your safety."

She released her breath and hurried for the Bronco. "You can tell him I'm fine."

As she turned right on the highway, her mind tried to take in the informer's words. If what he said was true, Sean was framed. And that meant whoever killed Officer Larson would not want the truth coming out. Claims of self-defense might be justified. But a cop killer? There would be no escaping justice.

Zane sped down the paved road in the minivan. The vehicle was not made for these fast speeds. The motorcycle had pulled out this way, but he hadn't seen his taillights since he'd turned. Where did the guy go? As he continued down the pavement, keeping a watch on the ditches and side roads, he wondered if the guy had pulled off somewhere and cut his lights.

He'd been going fast enough to whip right past him.

His cell phone rang, and he answered. "I haven't found him yet."

"Did you hear everything?" Bliss's voice came through the speaker with background noise.

"Yes, I did. We need this guy's name." Zane came to a T in the road and looked both directions. There were no lights either way. He took a left away from town. "Where are you going?"

"Still trying to find this guy. He could be a major key to who shot Larson."

Zane wasn't familiar with this area but had noticed a sign back there. "I'm on Sperry Road."

"Okay. I'm on County Road 312 headed north."

For the next fifteen minutes, they zigzagged over the back roads, but neither caught sight of the informer. When they admitted defeat, they met back at the Shake and Cake.

Zane exited his truck and walked over to Bliss's window. "What are your plans?"

"If you could drop me off at my house, I'll get my Tahoe and go by the hospital to check on our kidnapper. If he wakes up even for a bit, he might tell us where Wyatt is at. I'm worried about a child being alone at night."

Zane tried not to think about the fear his grandson must be feeling. He prayed Wyatt was warm and safe. The informer's comment about hearing a gunshot kept returning to his mind. At first he thought the man meant he feared the shooter, but if that was the case, why not tell Bliss who the suspect was, even if anonymously? "I was wondering about our guy's comment about being afraid."

"What do you make of that?"

"I remember there was a house burglarized that night in the neighborhood. Investigators first believed it might have had something to do with the shooting but ruled it out because there didn't seem to be a connection—one being a theft and the other a shooting of a cop."

"You think our informer was stealing that night?"

"Yeah, I do. I'll check the records, but I figure the complaint came from Throckmorton. The man not wanting his wife and kids to find out what a dumb mistake he'd made as a teenager is understandable. He would've been afraid of being arrested if he'd gone to the police."

"That makes sense."

"I'll meet you back at the center, and then I'll drop you off at your house."

"Okay. At least we have something now."

But would it be enough? The leads were trickling in too slow. The best thing that could happen would be for Lawrence to tell them where Wyatt was being kept. He could only pray the man would regain consciousness and tell them where his grandson was hidden.

FIFTEEN

Besides the glow from machines hooked up to Lawrence Weaver, little light filtered through the edges of the shades of the hospital room. Muted voices occasionally carried down the hall near the nurses' station, along with the buzzing of blood pressure cuffs every ten minutes.

Nighttime in the hospital gave Bliss time to think, which wasn't a good thing. She felt better when she was actively searching for Wyatt, but against her wishes, she had to admit the pain in her leg had grown worse, making it difficult to keep going.

She watched the man in bed who was desperate enough to steal a child in hopes of saving his brother. Stubble lined his face, and his coloring held a yellow hue. His chest went up and down with each breath. The memory of him yelling at her to stop because he didn't want to shoot her kept running through her mind.

Was he for real, or had that been just a ploy to keep her guessing?

How desperate did you have to be to kidnap someone? A couple of calls, and Bliss had learned Lawrence had made several attempts to get his brother's case reopened. He'd been persistent when his brother was first arrested, but after the sentencing, he'd seemed to settle back into his life. But the last seventeen months, he had made multiple new attempts to get the case reopened, even hiring a private investigator. Hansen Investigations had a reputation of not being a good company but were cheaper than most. Saul Hansen had gone from one small-town police department to another until he finally struck out on his own. Bliss wasn't certain what the man's problem was, but he couldn't stay employed for long.

She had already used her iPad to do more research and had called Josie Hunt to get an update to see how the investigation into Ike Harris was going. There didn't seem to be any connection between Ike and Sean. Josie and Chasity were also looking into drug arrests six months prior to and after Sean's arrest in the county. Since the Liberty PD were able to get a judge to sign off on a search warrant, there had to be evidence of drug deals. If Lawrence was right and he wasn't involved, then who was dealing?

So many questions but not much time to investigate. Her team needed to prioritize. Time was running out.

The door to the room swung open, and a nurse came in. She checked the patient's vitals and then looked up at Bliss. "I need to check the wound. Can you please step out into the hall?"

"Sure." As soon as she got to her feet, her thigh tightened. She guessed it wouldn't hurt to stretch her legs anyway. Her stomach had been growling the last hour, so she made her way to the elevator and down to the first floor. There were a couple of vending machines on every other floor, but the ones in the cafeteria contained more options than candy bars or nuts.

She bought herself a coffee and an apple, not exactly a tasty combination, but she'd feel better than if she ate something sugary or processed.

A glance to her cell phone showed no missed calls or texts. Frustration bit at her. What was Zane doing? She'd hoped for an update, even if there'd been nothing important to report. The waiting was excruciating.

She headed back up to the third floor. Normally, she would take the stairs, but she didn't think that was smart with her thigh hurting and took the elevator. When the doors opened, she stepped off and saw the nurse who'd checked on Lawrence disappear down another hall. At least she could go back into the room.

When Bliss stepped in, she was surprised to see Lawrence's eyes open and watching her.

"You're awake."

"I don't feel good." He squinted and stared for a moment. "What are you doing here?"

"I wanted to ask you about Wyatt."

Confusion etched across his face. "You're the lady from the island." It wasn't a question. His hands went to his chest, and his fingers prodded at the bandage. "What happened? Did you shoot me?"

"No. Someone else did. I'd like to know where the boy is and who shot you." At his narrowed brow, she decided to explain more. "You were found at the cemetery. But you were already injured when we arrived. Your truck was there, but not Wyatt. Where is Lieutenant Adcock's grandson?"

His eyes squinted and he heaved a breath, struggling. He clutched his chest. "I remember." He gasped. "Get the doc—"

An alarm on one of his machines made one continuous beep. Bliss looked on as the numbers flashed on the screen, followed by a flat line.

Footsteps ran up the hallway, and a nurse flew into the room. She hit an electronic device. "Code blue. Code blue in room three-twenty-two." Her gaze went to Bliss. "You need to step out."

She took one last glance at Lawrence. His face was turning blue. A man wearing scrubs ran past her and into the room. As she stepped into the hall, she could barely make out what they were saying in their hurried speech, but it didn't look good.

Just as she withdrew her cell phone to call Zane, the door to the stairs slammed. Instinct more than anything told her someone was leaving the scene. Ignoring her injured leg, she ran down the hall and went to the stairwell. Footsteps hurried below her. She took off while keeping an ear for silence, evidence the person had stopped and was waiting for her.

"Oh. Oh." She couldn't help but mumble the words to herself and her tender flesh rebelled against the quick movement. A glance into the door at the second floor showed no one in sight. She hurried down to the first floor with her gun in her grip. Again no one, so she continued to the parking garage. Through the diamond-patterned glass on the door, she spotted someone in a dark blue shirt disappearing behind a concrete pillar.

She hit Zane's number on her cell phone, but it went straight to voicemail. "I'm at the hospital. Lawrence may be in cardiac arrest. I'm in pursuit of the possible suspect."

As she clicked off, she realized the message was jumbled, but she trusted Zane would catch the gist.

She stepped out and allowed the door to slowly shut. No movement or sound presented itself. Easing herself along the wall, she made her way to a pillar that was three away from where the person disappeared.

Movement to her right had her turning in that direction. Still not having a visual, she moved silently to the next pillar. And then the next. Her grip tightened on her gun, and she moved it into position. She stepped to the next pillar—the one the person had gone behind. Swiftly, she stepped out.

Nobody was there.

She looked around for the man. The parking garage was more than three-quarters empty of vehicles, which meant there wasn't a good line of protection. Leaning low, she hurried across to a blue sedan that was on the far wall. Using the wall as protection, she continued along until she was halfway across.

The door to the hospital opened and shut. A middle-aged man emerged, talking on his cell phone. "…stop at the store and pick you up some drinks. I'll be home soon."

Alert for the possible suspect to make his move, she waited while the man made his way across to a black roadster. The vehicle started and the man backed out of his space. As he made his way down the aisle, his headlights illuminated a guy running. Bliss took off.

The car pulled out of the garage, but she kept on the move in the direction the man went. When she got to the edge, she glanced around but didn't see him. Her cell phone rang. "I may have lost him."

Zane said, "I'm on my way."

As she disconnected, something moved to her right

and disappeared behind some hedges. She couldn't let him get away.

The lawn outside the garage was dimly lit, and she hurried across. Once again, she caught sight of movement. The figure made an all-out dash for the street.

Taking the chance she wouldn't trip or step in a hole in the dark, she ran to catch him. The man got into a white midsize SUV and slammed the door. Bliss turned up the street. She'd parked just a few spaces down from the man.

She had her car in gear and moving before her door closed. Tires squealed as she peeled out. She placed her gun in her ankle holster so it wouldn't wind up on the floor. The SUV made a left turn onto a residential street. After she made the turn, she tried to call Zane back, but he didn't answer. Her car hit a dip and came back down with a jolt. At these fast speeds, she slid her cell phone under her right leg. The SUV took another left, and she followed it. He was increasing his distance.

She couldn't lose this guy.

Her cell phone buzzed, and Zane's name appeared on her car's screen. She answered it on Bluetooth.

"Where are you?"

"Pursuing the suspect. White SUV—can't tell what model. Don't know what street I'm on, but we're headed toward Hospital Hill." The hill was known to people in the area because of its steep incline. During the winter, the road was closed.

"I'm headed your way."

"Okay. Can you call this in so we can take this guy down? I don't want him to get away this time."

"I'm on it."

"Okay." She pushed the disconnect button on her steering wheel just as she came to a sharp curve. Hitting her brakes, she slid around the turn. Her vehicle was too high-profile to hug the road like the guy's smaller SUV. He was willing to drive faster than her, and she had to ask herself if she was willing to push harder.

As they neared the edge of town, she increased her speed. Thankfully, few cars were on the road, and her foot pressed the gas even more. A car sluggishly pulled out of a twenty-four-hour convenience store, and she whipped around him without slowing. She was gaining on the suspect.

Her thigh ached, but victory was so close, she couldn't be distracted. Since the man was in the hospital room, she didn't think Wyatt was with him. If so, she would never put him in danger.

Not a red light or intersection in sight, only open highway. She accelerated. The need for speed had never appealed to her, and her heart raced with the car. A blowout or something discarded in the road could be enough to kill her at this rate, and she paid attention to what her headlights reflected off. The landscape thinned out into farming country. Several pastures of cattle grazed.

As soon as this guy stopped, she could learn where Wyatt had been hidden. She couldn't fail. Then Zane could start mending the relationship with Sage. Something she truly wanted to see happen. And if Sean was innocent of shooting Officer Larson, then she prayed they'd find the true killer in time to save the man from execution.

Her gas light dinged. "Oh. Not now." Surely the chase would be over before she ran out. The SUV made a series of turns down paved country roads. Its brake lights flashed as he slowed for a T in the road. *Please, Lord, help us not to wreck.*

Did she dare try to ram him? No. These roads were too rough, especially difficult to maneuver at night. It'd be safer to follow him until he crashed or finally grew tired and pulled over.

Her phone buzzed again. "This is Bliss."

"You still with our man?"

"Yeah. We're headed east on the back roads and just turned onto Bokchito Road. I think he's trying to lose me, but I'm hanging on."

"I'm still a few miles behind you, but I'll stick to the highway and see if I can get ahead of you. The police are on their way. I want you to be careful. If you need to back off…"

"I'm not going to wreck. I want this guy. Have you heard from the hospital? Did Lawrence make it?"

"Don't know anything yet. Dryden is there now, but the doctors are still working on him."

The road went up a steep hill, and a sharp curve stood at the top. She held tight as she swung wide, trying to keep her tires on the road. Her car dipped into the ditch, and her heart stampeded. Mud kicked up, spraying her windows. A gasp escaped her before she drove straight until she could get the car back on the pavement.

"What's going on?"

"I need to pay attention. Stay on the line, and I'll let you know if our suspect changes directions." After he affirmed, her mind struggled to remember what was out here. Just farms that she could recall.

The pavement ended, and the white SUV turned right. "He's getting on Highway 72."

"I'm almost there now."

"We're coming up to Bokchito Livestock Auction." She barely got the words out when an oncoming semi-truck pulling a cattle trailer went to turn in front of them. "Watch out!"

She cringed as the SUV jerked to the right, and he tried to miss the truck. The vehicle went off the road and fishtailed before the truck slammed into it, shoving it into the auction's drive. Sparks flew as it smashed the smaller vehicle into half its size. "Oh no."

"What's going on?"

Instead of stopping, the big rig kept the gas down, pushing the SUV across the parking lot and against the metal pipe corral. Black smoke rose from the exhaust as the SUV was smashed flat.

"What is wrong with the guy?" Her blood pounded through her veins and throbbed in her ears.

Headlights headed up the highway toward her. "I'm almost there." Zane's pickup whipped into the parking lot.

The rig backed up and then black smoke bellowed as the driver hit the gas. It peeled out of the drive, barely missing Zane. She looked for the license plate on the back of the rig, but it was missing.

Zane pulled up beside her, and they both jumped out of their vehicles at the same time.

His gaze caught hers. "Are you all right?"

"Yeah." Her gaze fixed on the SUV. "But I don't think our suspect is. Are you going after the semi?"

"No. The man from the hospital is more important. Call for an ambulance."

"Zane, that was no accident."

"I know. And now we know there is more than one person involved."

SIXTEEN

With one look at the SUV, Zane knew they'd need to get the Jaws of Life to get the suspect out. He called Ranger O'Neill, who informed him he was less than two minutes away.

A couple of people ran out from the auction building. Sirens sounded in the distance. A few minutes later, paramedics pulled into the drive, followed by an ambulance. A man and a woman jumped out, and then the man grabbed the Jaws of Life.

Zane stepped back and gave the people room to work.

Ranger O'Neill arrived at the scene and gave a low whistle as he approached. "That's some major damage."

Zane updated his ranger on the situation, and they talked on and off as they watched. Dryden called to let him know Lawrence had survived the attack but was in critical condition. He quickly relayed the information to Bliss, who merely stared off into the distance.

It seemed to take forever to cut through the mangled mess of metal. Because of the condition of the SUV, they had to go through the roof instead of the door. A hard pit formed in his stomach. He didn't see how anyone could survive the accident, but a person never knew.

Chief Cunningham arrived and talked with one of the medics before heading toward Zane. They all talked in hushed tones, seemingly with little hope, but no one said the words.

After twenty minutes, one of the paramedics walked over. "The driver didn't make it."

Bliss leaned against the front of her vehicle and stared at the wrecked SUV.

Zane strode over to tell Bliss the driver was dead.

"I thought so. Did you recognize him?"

He shook his head. "No."

Distress was written on her face, and her arms were folded across her chest like she had a chill. "I don't get it. How did the driver of the big rig know our suspect was on this road?"

"I was wondering the same thing."

"The SUV driver had to let someone know he was on this road because the semitruck came from the opposite direction." She turned to leave. "I'm going back to the hospital."

"It's dangerous. I'll send Dryden or O'Neill to stay there with you."

She sighed. "I'd appreciate that. I'll catch you later."

As he stared at her retreating back, he yelled, "Hold up. I want to go with you."

She glanced over her shoulder. "Someone has to know something. It stands to reason Lawrence knows who shot him, and it's the same person who killed Officer Larson."

"We'll keep a twenty-four-hour watch over him."

She nodded and got into her vehicle. "I need to stop for gas."

"Okay." As Zane pulled out behind her, he called

Dryden. "I need you to stay at the hospital to watch over Lawrence."

"Are you certain? I want to follow up a lead from the original case."

"What lead?" Law enforcement was spread too thin, and he still had no idea where his grandson was being kept. Time was running out.

"Chasity called about a drug dealer, Peyton Fehan, from years ago who could have a possible connection to Sean Weaver. If we could tie up one part of the case, we could all concentrate on finding your grandson instead."

"We don't know the driver of the semitruck, but it'd be too convenient for the shooter outside of Lawrence's residence and the one who shot him at the cemetery to also happen to drive a big rig. I think we have more than one man. I'll be at the hospital in a bit, and we'll get a couple of the local police officers to watch over our man." After Zane disconnected, he thought about who to trust in security. It'd have to be someone hired less than sixteen years ago, someone who had no connections to the Weaver-Larson case.

Forty minutes later, after he pumped her gas, Zane met Bliss in the hospital parking lot. A heavy dew hung in the air. Normally, he'd never hover over someone on his team, but he wasn't taking any chances with Bliss.

"Are you okay?"

She walked in stride with him, even though her limp didn't seem as pronounced. "You keep asking me that. I'll let you know if I need something."

"I just worry…"

She held her hand in the air. "My leg is killing me. I'm exhausted from lack of sleep and too much adren-

aline from all the dangerous adventures. Emotionally,
I'm all over the place. The more I get my hopes up
that we're onto a solid lead, the harder the punch when
everything comes tumbling down. But I've been in
dark places before, and I assume I'm no worse off than
you. Quit babying me. It gets on my nerves."

He laughed. "I'd forgotten how much I missed you.
Forgive me for being concerned." She was right. Except
for the gunshot wound, he was exactly in the same boat.

As soon as they stepped into the Intensive Care Unit,
they were stopped by a nurse. "Visiting hours are not
until six a.m. You must return then."

Zane pointed to his badge. "We're here to check on
Lawrence Weaver, ma'am."

"Still not allowed. You can wait outside in the hall.
Better yet, there's a waiting room down the hall with
coffee."

Bliss intervened. "Can we talk with a doctor?"

A curtain to a room on the left was partially open.
Lawrence lay in a bed hooked up to several machines.
A lady in a white coat was in his room.

"I'll send her out when she can, but I don't know
how long that will be."

"Thanks," both Bliss and Zane said in unison.

When they stepped out, he said, "You have your
weapon with you?"

"Of course."

"Would you like a cup of coffee?"

"I would love some."

The coffeepot was almost empty and looked dark,
like it'd been sitting there a long time. After he put on
a fresh pot, he grabbed a plastic chair and carried it to
Bliss in the hallway.

"Thank you. My feet are killing me." She sat and glanced at his hands questioningly.

"I dumped the coffee and am brewing some now."

She nodded and then rubbed her face in her hands. "Don't you want to sit?"

"No, I'm good." He had too much frustrated adrenaline rushing through him.

"I wonder how long it would take to learn if someone administered a drug to Lawrence to make him go into a spell. It's too coincidental for him to flatline right after someone ran out of here."

"Yeah. And then that person was hit by a semitruck." There was nothing more torturous than waiting when his grandson was in danger. Hurry up and wait. The never-ending cycle of an officer's life. Bouts of danger followed by drawn-out periods of waiting, tedious searching for evidence or filling out paperwork.

The door to the ICU opened and a fiftyish woman stepped out. "I'm Dr. Morimura. Are you the Texas Ranger asking about Mr. Weaver?" At his nod, she asked, "What can I help you with?"

Bliss got to her feet.

"My partner was here when Weaver had a setback. She heard someone running who escaped down the stairs. Have you found evidence of tampering with the patient?"

"Like being given an injection or a drug?" The doctor's gaze narrowed.

"Could be. Anything that could have caused the episode besides the liver cancer or the gunshot wound."

"I've been told our patient was potentially involved in some kind of crime and then was shot. Our job is to administer medical care, but we still must protect the patient's privacy."

Bliss stepped forward. "Can you tell us if you've examined him to see if anything unnatural contributed to the episode?"

The doctor's gaze flitted to Bliss before returning to him. "We're running a series of tests, but the labs could take a day or longer. Is there anything in particular you believe we should check for?"

Zane recalled the paperwork he'd looked through at Lawrence's home. "Penicillin. He was allergic to it."

"We have not, but we'll look into it." Her gaze narrowed again, but she didn't comment on Lawrence being allergic to the antibiotic. "That's all I can promise."

"I appreciate it."

The doctor left them standing in the hallway.

Bliss asked, "How did you know about the penicillin?"

"I saw it while going through his bills in his office."

A few minutes later, a door opened, and a Liberty uniformed officer approached them. Vawter was the name on his badge. "I'm here to stand guard at Weaver's door."

"Officer Vawter, can I ask how long you've been with the department?"

The man stiffened, and he frowned. "I've been in law enforcement for twenty years, but with the Liberty PD for five and a half years. Why?"

Zane purposely didn't answer the man's question. If he explained he didn't want anyone on the case who might have something to hide from Officer Larson's shooting, it would cause more defensiveness than the man exhibited right now. And he didn't want to tip off the true person behind the crime. "I'm sure you know this man's brother is scheduled to be executed in less than twenty-six hours."

"I was briefed."

"Good. I've always enjoyed working with the fine officers in our local departments."

Some of the tension dissolved as the man settled in the chair Bliss had vacated.

"How do you take your coffee?"

"Me?" Vawter asked. At Zane's nod, he said, "Two creamers."

"Come on, Bliss. Let's get you that coffee now." Zane jerked his head toward the waiting room.

"I can wait," she said.

"Humor me. I don't want anyone getting by this guy."

He filled a couple of cups and added creamer to the officer's.

Bliss leaned in and kept her voice low. "So, tell me more about the lead Dryden was following."

"A drug dealer by the name of Peyton Fehan. He was arrested a few months after Officer Larson's murder but only served five years. He'd been known to work Sean's neighborhood during those days."

"Anything else?" She took a sip.

Zane shrugged. "It may or may not be important, but he moved back to the area a few months ago."

"So, the reasoning would be if he was Larson's killer, he's trying to stop the investigation."

"Looks like it. Oh, and you mentioned the young officer thought he recognized our informant on the motorcycle."

"Yeah. Did he remember his identity?"

The corner of Zane's lips lifted. "He believes so. The preacher from over at First Liberty."

Her mouth dropped open. "That explains why he doesn't want anyone to know he was stealing years ago, even if he was a minor."

"Yeah. I would've hoped his conscience for seeing another suspect at Weaver's house would have pricked him more. Chasity is supposed to contact him tomorrow to see if we can get him to fess up. Back to our suspects. Besides Ike Harris, our list is short. Lawrence mentioned the Texas Rangers worked the case, and I need to learn who planted evidence."

"As in, he thought it was one of the rangers?"

He nodded. "I'm guessing a ranger or a police officer."

"Who helped you work the case?"

He stared at the ground. "Ranger Hale. He was the one who wrote the report you read. He was a twenty-year veteran on the team and was as straight as they come. I talked with my captain, and he's giving one of the investigators the task of going back through his record."

"*If* someone planted evidence, you don't believe it was him."

"No, I don't. But I don't want to overlook any suspects. We're running out of time."

They walked back to the guard, and Zane handed him the coffee. After the officer thanked them, they continued to the elevators.

Bliss turned to him. "Are you headed out to help Dryden interview the drug dealer?"

"Yeah. We just keep following the leads. Are you staying here or going home?"

"I'm staying here. I realize Lawrence's chances are slim, but I want to be here in case he comes around."

"I'll touch base with you in a little while." Zane tipped his hat to her and disappeared down the hall.

In a little while, the execution would be over. And if Lawrence didn't make it, Wyatt might not ever be found. Time had run out.

Frustration built as Zane made it to the parking lot and climbed into his truck. Criminals always left clues. They had to be overlooking something. From the grenade in the cellar to someone locking him and Bliss in the shipping containers, this had been a strange case.

There was a good chance Larson's killer was a law officer. The thought settled hard in his chest, and he'd like to believe those who promised to uphold laws were above such acts. At the end of the day, officers were people.

As he pulled onto the road, he called Dryden. "I've changed my mind. Time has run out. Can you handle your interview with Fehan?"

"I've got it handled. Are you onto a lead?"

"Not yet. But I'm backtracking our steps where Wyatt has been since his abduction. If I learn something, I'll let you know." After he disconnected, he called Captain Brewer to give him an update.

When he was done filling him in, the captain said, "We've thoroughly investigated Ranger Hale. All the evidence says he's clean."

"I'm glad to hear that."

"We haven't found out anything more on Cunningham or Richards. Carpenter was put on suspension for domestic violence accusations six years ago, but you already knew that. Sorry I don't have better news."

"That's fine. I knew you'd let me know." Zane hung up and turned on the highway to Lawrence's house, something nagging at him.

Jason Cunningham had a hunting photo on his office wall. Zane was only at his office a minute before learning they'd move their meetings to the community center.

The thought came to him suddenly, and he immediately pulled onto the shoulder of the road. He waited for a car to pass before he turned his truck around. As he sped down the highway, he couldn't get his mind off the hunting cabin with the grenades. The consensus had been the ambush had meant to kill him and Bliss, but it made no sense for someone to have planted the grenades.

Even at a fast speed, it took longer than he'd like to get to the hunting cabin.

Zane stopped in front of the containers and got out. Instead of searching through them, he hurried back to the shed. Investigators had already gone over most of the items, but mainly they were interested in the grenades. The box that contained the explosives was checked for fingerprints, but none were found.

Who wiped prints from a box of grenades? Someone who didn't want to be identified.

Some of the other items, like storage tubs and the gun, were checked. So far, all those prints had belonged to several different hunters, but none were on their suspect list. Two large ice chests sat on the top shelf, and he pulled them down. He removed the lid to the first and found a huge stack of folded camouflage shirts. The next tub contained a stack of framed pictures.

Bingo.

He flipped through them. The third one was what he was looking for. He stared down at Jason Cunningham's smiling face while he held up a large buck by the antlers. He must've either wiped his prints from the items or took what had belonged to him so he couldn't be traced back.

Zane took the photo and hurried back to his truck. They were going to get Larson's killer today and learn the location of his grandson. First, he needed to call Bliss to let her know what he'd found.

As her cell phone went to voicemail, his heart constricted. They'd just caught a big break, but he felt a strong sense of dread that this nightmare was far from over.

SEVENTEEN

Bliss sat opposite Lawrence's bed in a plastic chair. Blinking lights on the machine and the occasional sound of his blood pressure cuff filled the void of the silent room. Somewhere down the hall a couple of nurses talked quietly. She watched the kidnapper, hoping any moment he'd awake and start talking.

For the past two hours, she'd sat quietly, waiting, but he hadn't moved.

She'd worried about Wyatt, thought about Sean's case and wondered if they'd find evidence in time to stop the execution. If not, how would she deal with the knowledge she could've stopped an unjust killing if she could've moved faster?

Her eyes grew heavy, and even though she'd tried to catch a couple of winks, sleep wouldn't come. The waiting made her want to ride her row machine for an hour. Go for a run. Anything to expend restless energy. Sitting in a chair while Wyatt was missing brought back too many nights of Bliss waiting to hear about Mitchell.

She rolled her neck, trying to ease the tension.

It had been a lonely journey. One day, she had a husband and a child with the hope of more children coming. In a moment, everything she longed for had vanished.

Others had told her to move on and put that part of her life behind her. But how could she forget her family was gone? As the years passed, she now wondered if those people had been right. Fourteen years later, and it had been for naught.

And of all people, Zane Adcock had reached out and asked her to help find his grandson. She simply couldn't fathom how she would handle it if, like Mitchell, Wyatt never came home.

Movement caught her attention. Lawrence's hand rubbed his face, the IV line going with his arm.

She sat and watched him intently.

Just when she thought he'd gone back under, his eyes opened.

Getting to her feet, she stepped forward. "Lawrence, it's me, Bliss Walker. I don't know if you can understand me, but we're trying to find Wyatt, the boy you kidnapped. Where did you hide him?"

"Sean? Is he...?"

"His execution is not until tonight. He's still alive, and we know he was framed. We haven't found enough evidence, but we're close. Please, help me find the boy."

Lawrence opened his mouth to speak and licked his lips. "The shack."

"Where's the shack?"

He closed his eyes.

Seconds passed, and she feared he was out again.

"The place my daddy used to farm."

"Please. Help me. I need more to go on. Where is this?"

"Grown up. The old Hill place. North, north—" His gaze went over Bliss's head.

She turned around. The chief of police stood there,

his gaze connecting with hers. For several moments, they simply stared at one another.

"I came by to see how our kidnapper is doing." Jason stepped around her and up to the bed. "You appear to be doing better."

A dark feeling came over her. Bliss didn't like the way the chief was acting and didn't want to leave him alone with Lawrence. By the fear in the patient's eyes, he must have felt the same way. She glanced at the clock on the wall. "Visiting hours are over. I'll check back with you later."

She turned and put her hand on the chief's shoulder, and he flinched. She went on to say, "We better let him rest."

His gaze penetrated hers, and for a moment, she didn't know if he'd leave. But he finally said, "Of course. Rest."

She stepped into the hall first, with Jason right behind her. Thankfully, Officer Vawter was standing outside. No doubt the chief could easily command the officer to step aside. She stared at him until he noticed the intensity. "Take good care of our patient."

She stared hard, and he blinked. Confusion etched in his eyebrows. "I will."

Before she walked away, she gave him one more warning look. As she stepped onto the elevator, an arm stopped the doors from closing, and Jason stepped inside. Tension as thick as maple syrup on a cold day filled the confining space.

It wasn't in her to display nervousness, no matter how much her stomach was in knots. Wyatt needed to be rescued. Just because the chief was acting strange didn't mean he was guilty of a crime, but she couldn't shake the feeling.

Why did he jump when she touched his shoulder, like he was injured? The suspect at her house had been shot. She looked him in the eyes, and she knew—the chief was the one targeting them.

They still needed evidence.

He smiled and his brilliant white teeth sparkled. "I appreciate your team helping with this case. What's your next step?"

"To keep searching until we find the missing child." The door opened. "And to aid law enforcement in all ways we can to bring down the perpetrator."

"Sounds like a hazardous job. I'm certain I don't have to tell you to be careful."

The temptation to spout a warning to him crossed her mind, but she didn't handle herself with threats. She'd learned a long time ago the truth to the old adage "actions speak louder than words." And she intended to rescue Wyatt and help bring justice to those involved in the crime—even if it happened to be a chief of police.

As soon as she was safely in her Tahoe, she punched in Zane's number. Three rings and it went to voicemail. She left a message to call her. And then she dialed Josie. "I need your help. I might be onto something. I hope you can help me find a shack with little to go on. It's north of Liberty and the landowner's or former landowner's name is Hill."

She prayed Hill was the name and not a description of the place. Because she was running out of ideas of how to rescue the child.

Zane tried to call Bliss, but when she didn't answer, he punched Josie's number. When she answered, he asked, "Do you know where Bliss is? She left a voice-mail but is not answering."

"Not exactly, but I know the area. She's north of Liberty off Farm Road 215. She's looking for a shack in between that highway and Lickety-Split Road."

"Thanks. And, Josie, if you hear from her, tell her not to go near the chief of police."

"She asked me to dig into his background, so I'd say you two are thinking alike. And, Lieutenant, please be careful."

Bliss, if you suspect the chief, please keep your distance.

Zane hurried through Liberty and talked to his rangers on the phone, telling them their suspect was Jason Cunningham. As he sped down the road, he realized how scared he was to not only lose Wyatt but Bliss, too.

His cell rang and Bliss's number showed on the screen. "Where are you?"

"Cell reception is terrible out here. I'm at the Hill place. Didn't you get my message?"

"Yeah. I think Cunningham is our cop killer."

"Oh, Zane…" Static filled the line, and then the call dropped. Three minutes later, he saw the sign for Lickety-Split, and a large grove of trees stood in the distance. He pulled into the dirt drive and followed it back until he spotted Bliss's Tahoe and a shack that was barely standing behind that.

He let out a breath and pulled up beside her vehicle.

"I just got here." She approached him. "Lawrence indicated Wyatt was here. But he struggled to speak, so I'm not certain where your grandson is. I've been calling him, but there's no answer." She glanced up. "Oh no."

"What?" He turned around, and a huge dust cloud kicked up on Farm Road 215 behind a black Liberty Police Ford pickup—the kind the chief drove.

"Do you think that's the chief?"

"Maybe. And we're not taking a chance." Zane drew his weapon. "Go find Wyatt while I stand guard." When she hesitated, he repeated, "Go."

"Be careful." She took off.

He hadn't come this far to back down now.

EIGHTEEN

The dilapidated homestead was surrounded by trees, so the home was barely visible. A rusty windmill turned in the breeze, creating a loud creaking sound.

Bliss hurried up the rotting steps into the shack. Dank air greeted her. "Wyatt, where are you? I'm here to help you."

A mouse skittered in the walls and a branch grated against the window. Careful not to step on the broken planks, she made her way through the house, checking the rooms and closets. "Wyatt, I'm here to take you to your mama. If you hear me, please come out."

Besides the rodents and who knew what other things, she heard nothing else. The back door stood open with a pile of leaves at its base. The screen door slacked on the hinges, and she exited onto a small porch. A glance toward their vehicles showed Zane leaning against the hood of his truck with his gun aimed as Cunningham's truck neared the property's entrance.

Outside were two more buildings that she hurried to check out. One was a tool shed and the other looked to be an ancient smokehouse, but neither showed signs of Wyatt. She stepped back out.

He had to be here.

She called his name again, and she noticed Zane looking her way. She held her hands in the air, indicating she hadn't found him yet. Continuing deeper into the woods, she tried again. "Wyatt. Are you here?"

The faint cry of a child reached her.

"Zane, I hear him! Wyatt's here!" She headed toward the sound as she searched the woods. Her gaze landed on an old brick circle. Oh no. A well. She ran to the crumbling mass of stone and looked over the edge.

A dark-haired little boy looked at her. Thankfully, the well was dry and a rope ladder lay on the ground.

"I found him!"

A gunshot split the air as Jason Cunningham's truck whipped into the drive, bouncing over the rugged terrain.

Zane returned fire. She trusted him to hold off the chief while she grabbed the boy.

"I'm going to get you out of there, Wyatt. Here comes the ladder." She carefully let down the rope so it wouldn't hit or startle him. The other end was tied to the large trunk of a pecan tree, and she gave it a good tug to make certain it wouldn't break.

More gunfire exploded.

She took one last glance over her shoulder to see Jason's truck ram Zane's before she climbed over the edge. She trusted him to do his job.

Please, Lord, keep Zane safe.

As she went down the cold side of the well, a spiderweb stuck to her arm, but she kept descending into the dark hole. When she reached the bottom, the boy moved against the side away from her.

"Wyatt. It's okay. I came to help you. My name is Bliss." She held out her hands to him, but he frowned

and cried. What could she say since she had him in
her arms on the island? No wonder he didn't trust her.
"I'm going to get us out of here."

He stopped crying and looked at her.

"Come on. I know you're scared." She scooped him
up into her arms and paused a second to make certain
he wouldn't fight her. He threw his arms around her
neck, the warmth of his little body soaking into hers.
Moisture lined her eyes as she embraced him in a hug.
"Let's get out of here."

She grabbed the rung above her head with her free
hand and then put her foot on the bottom rung. It was
tricky to climb while the ladder swung with each step,
but she held tight and worked her way upward.

Wyatt's grasp was strong, and he looked up as they
struggled their way to the top. Finally, she was just
about to pull herself up to the edge when a shadow
passed over them.

Jason Cunningham's face appeared above them.
Blood smeared the man's cheek, and mud matted his
hair. "Not so fast. I hate to do this, but you leave me no
choice."

A knife appeared in his hand, and then he was cut-
ting the rope.

"No! Let us out of here." Afraid of falling, Bliss
hurried down the ladder before he finished his mission. Her boot slid through the rung, and then they
swung hard into the wall, her shoulder taking most of
the brunt. One side must've been cut, because her right
hand dipped suddenly. She took another step before
they fell to the ground, landing on her feet, but pro-
pelled forward and slammed into the side of the well.
The rope landed next to her.

Wyatt cried. "I want out. I want to see my mama."

She glanced up and saw daylight, but there was no sign of Jason. "I've still got you, Wyatt. I'm not letting you go, honey."

Limbs blew above the well opening, and then the faint rumblings of thunder.

She swallowed down the temptation to call out to Zane. Realization settled heavy on her. If he was all right, Jason would've never made it to them.

How was she going to get this child out of here?

Every muscle in Zane's body throbbed with pain as he tried to get out from underneath his mangled truck. His head swam, and it felt like he'd hyperextended his left arm. Jason had rammed his truck, and Zane hadn't been able to get out of the way until the vehicle practically ran him over.

One of his shots may have hit the chief. He couldn't be sure. Was Bliss still in the well? He had to find her and his grandson.

He struggled to his feet and stumbled forward before catching himself. He moved toward the woods when he spotted blood. And more drops appeared. Even though dizziness still threatened, he hurried to the well. Over to the side, Jason lay facedown on the ground. One of Zane's bullets must've hit him, or Cunningham was injured when their vehicles crashed.

Zane didn't have time to help him right now, but he removed the knife from his hand and checked him for other weapons, not finding any. When he looked over the side of the well, his gaze fell on Bliss with a small boy. He never had been so glad to see anyone in his life!

"Zane. I'm so glad you're all right. Get us out of here."

"Hold on. I have a tie strap in the back of my truck." He hurried to his vehicle to retrieve it and left Jason's knife in his console. As he hurried back with the strap, he called Dryden and let him know their location.

He glanced around. Jason was gone. He scouted a few feet in the woods to see if he was close but didn't see him. He would find him in a minute after Bliss and Wyatt were out of the well.

"Here it comes. Watch out for the metal hook." He lowered the strap down. "Wrap it around yourself, and I'll pull you up."

"Okay. Give me a second." She set Wyatt on the ground and put it around her midsection, creating a seat. She gathered the boy in her arms.

Zane watched to make certain she had a good hold. "Hang on."

Even though his muscles were hurting, he pulled on the strap as Bliss stepped on the narrow lips created by the rows of bricks to assist while keeping an eye out for Jason. The chief was nowhere in sight. When Bliss was near the top, Zane reached in and took Wyatt from her and then gave her a hand the rest of the way up.

Brown eyes stared intently at him, and his heart melted. "Wyatt." He stopped to clear his throat from the emotion.

The boy stopped and looked up at him, his brown eyes meeting his. "Who are you?"

"Zane Adcock." Had Sage told her son about him?

"Is that a gun?" Wyatt pointed to the one on his waist.

"Yes, it is." He didn't want the boy to be excited about a gun. "I'm a Texas Ranger, kind of like a police officer. I'm trained to use a gun."

His eyes grew large. "Really? A Texas Ranger? You

look like a cowboy. My grandpa is a Texas Ranger. He gets the bad guys."

Zane and Bliss exchanged glances.

Sage must've told her son about him. "Wyatt, *I'm* your grandpa."

"You are? You look different."

Bliss glanced at Zane before she asked Wyatt, "Different from what?"

"The picture on my mama's desk. She showed it to me. It's a picture of her with her mom, dad and a little white dog. She let me take it to school on Grandparents' Day."

Zane nodded and gave him a squeeze. "We're taking you to your mama. Okay?"

"Okay." A grin broke out on his face. "Are you a cowboy?"

Zane laughed. "Yep. You could say that."

"Do you have a horse?"

"I do. I'll let you ride sometime if your mama says it's okay. Would you like that?"

"Yeah!"

Bliss stared at him with tears in her eyes.

It'd been so long since he'd held a child. "Do you want to take him?"

"You go ahead." She glanced around. "Hey. Where's the chief?"

"I'm not certain, but he's injured. He was bleeding and on the ground a few minutes ago. I took his knife and searched for more weapons. Keep alert. Dryden, Randolph and O'Neill are on their way here."

"I'll be glad when Jason is behind bars."

"Me too."

The weight lifted from his shoulders as he carried

the boy toward his truck. He hoped now that he'd met Wyatt, he and Sage could mend their relationship. He'd love to spend time with his grandson. Zane had fond memories of his own granddad.

Bliss stopped. "The chief's truck is gone."

He looked to where the pickup had been. "I'll tell my rangers to be on the lookout."

The back end of Zane's truck was smashed, but he didn't think it would stop it from running. He turned the ignition. The engine fired right up. Zane grabbed his cell phone and called Dryden. "Cunningham just left here in his truck. He's injured. Don't let him get past you."

"We're fifteen minutes away, so we'll set up tack strips in both directions to cut him off."

"That's good. But I also want a chopper in the air."

Dryden hesitated, and Zane figured he was wondering if the helicopter was necessary, but he didn't want to voice his opinion. "I don't want to take chances on our man getting away. He's desperate and has been hiding the murder of Officer Larson for sixteen years. He won't be thinking clearly."

"Yes, sir. Will do."

Zane clicked off.

"Do you need to go after him, Zane? I can wait here with Wyatt until Jason is apprehended."

He didn't have to think about it. "No. You two are staying with me. I'll lead the way and you follow. I'm making sure this young man gets back to his mama."

"I agree."

"Let's go." He buckled Wyatt in the center seat of Bliss's Tahoe.

Both of them scrambled to get in their vehicles.

His truck squeaked, and a back tire rubbed on the fender, but he could take it to the body shop later. He pulled out on the country road while keeping an eye out for Jason's vehicle.

The skies were dark, but at least it wasn't raining.

Zane glanced in his mirror. He couldn't be certain, but it looked like Bliss was talking to his grandson. His heart hurt for what she had lost the day her son disappeared. He'd never seen her around children, but he could imagine she was a caring mom.

His mind switched gears to Jason Cunningham. What would he do now that the news he'd set up Sean Weaver was getting around? It wouldn't benefit him to hurt him or Bliss, so he was probably on the run. That was what Zane would do.

They had to cross the dam to get to the highway back to Liberty, but the water level was high, even though the floodgates were open. Water rushed out of the gates, and whitecaps showed all over the place.

Suddenly, a vehicle appeared behind Bliss in his rearview mirror and was coming quickly. He called her on his cell phone, and she answered on the first ring. "Hang on. We have company."

"Is that the chief?"

"No. Cunningham's pickup is black. I don't recognize it, but it's coming too fast." Zane let off the gas. He didn't want to take the chance of Wyatt or Bliss getting hurt. "Pass me."

"Okay." Her Tahoe switched lanes and flew by him.

The white pickup truck slammed into his back bumper, causing him to fishtail.

"Are you all right?"

He got his truck back under control. "Get over the

dam. The rangers will be here any minute to help me. I want you out of the way."

With the white truck following him, he'd taken his eyes off Bliss. He looked up, and Cunningham's black truck was headed straight at her from the opposite direction. "Watch out!"

Her Tahoe jerked to the right, but it was too late. Cunningham rammed her hard. Her front tire blew, sending her out of control toward the railing.

The chief continued to push.

"Zane, help us!" Their screams came over the speaker as both of the vehicles crashed through the barrier and bounced down the steep incline.

His chest squeezed, and he gripped his own steering wheel as if his effort could stop them.

They hit water, and the back door flew open on impact.

Water poured in.

He slammed on his brakes and jumped out of his truck. He aimed his weapon at the driver of the white truck, but the driver sped away.

He ran to the side of the road and looked on. Bliss was trying to unbuckle Wyatt. But her SUV was flowing fast toward the swirling water of the vortex.

NINETEEN

The impact had Bliss disoriented, but survival instincts kicked in as she rushed to get Wyatt out of the vehicle. Once she had him in her arms, the tilting Tahoe had her sliding out of the seat and into the rushing waters.

She struggled to get his head out of the water, but she was carried in the rush, out of control. She bobbed as she moved fast toward the vortex.

"Bliss!" Zane's voice could barely be heard over the loud rumble of moving water.

In front of her, Cunningham's truck quickly went downstream.

Please, Lord, save us.

After all the searching and trying to find Wyatt, had it all been for naught?

She kicked and moved her free arm while keeping a tight grip on Wyatt. The boy cried and clung to her, choking her.

The chief's vehicle suddenly went toward the middle of the stream, straight toward the massive whirlpool. Like pulling the plug out of the bathtub drain, water churned like an angry downward tornado. She could see Jason kicking the window, evidently trying unsuccessfully to break out the glass.

But she didn't have time to worry about the cop killer, for she also began to be sucked into the giant swirl.

"Bliss!"

She swiveled to Zane, who was running along the side of the river, something in his hand. He dived into the stream and immediately went under. Dryden and Randolph were on the bank, but she lost sight of them as she was swept closer to the vortex.

In horror, she watched Jason's truck be sucked into the vortex and spiral out of control until it spun deeper and quicker.

Then his truck vanished from sight.

Her heart raced as she tried to swim away from the vortex, but it did no good. The rush was too powerful. Wyatt continued to cry in her arm, but she retained a tight grip. She wouldn't give up this fight.

Zane appeared in front of her, a rope attached to his safety vest. He held his hand out to her.

She reached for him but was swept away in the unforgiving current. *No!*

The whirlpool pushed her quickly away from the lieutenant and onto the other side of the swirling hole. Her body was fraught with exhaustion, and she didn't know how much longer she could hold on. She'd never been a great swimmer, and she used too much energy to keep her head above water. But she couldn't give up now. As she continued to go around the vortex, she figured she had one more shot as she passed by the side of the road.

Again, she was sucked under the surface, and she battled to get her head above water. Wyatt coughed and gagged. As her energy waned, she knew it was impossible. She couldn't save both Wyatt and herself.

The current sucked her back around, but this time in a tighter circle. In the bouncing up and down, her gaze fell on Ranger Dryden. She drew near and tried to pull Wyatt from her grasp so she could hand him off, but the boy desperately clung to her and cried.

At the last second, he was pulled from her arms. Even as she tried to keep her head up, it was no use.

The swirling water tugged her deeper.

Suddenly, a hand grabbed her arm. The current kept pulling her, but the grip remained strong. For a brief moment, she surfaced and saw Zane's face as he struggled to hold her, the current pulling them until the rope was tight.

Please, Lord, save us. Don't let Zane drown trying to save me.

The vortex relentlessly tugged at them, and she was afraid the rope would snap.

"Hang on." Zane's grip on her repositioned as he wrapped his arm around her shoulders from behind.

She leaned her head back and saw sky. Inhaling a deep breath made her cough.

But then they were moving farther away from the powerful drain. The ranger's hold remained persistent as they got farther away from the vortex.

Suddenly, her feet touched the ground, and Zane turned her around.

She stared into his dark eyes, water dripping from his face and concern etched across his brow.

"Are…?" He took a deep breath. "Are you okay?"

"Yes." She fell against his chest. He wrapped his arms around her, and his chin rested on the top of her head. For several seconds, they clung to one another.

Without breaking contact, he said, "I've never been so scared of losing anyone in my life. I'm so glad you're not hurt."

She swallowed. "Where's Wyatt? Is he safe?"

"Yes, ma'am." Ranger Randolph stepped beside her. "Let's get you two out of here."

Her muscles trembled, and she fell, but Zane helped her back to her feet. Between the two rangers, she made it out of the water and back to dry land. She spotted Wyatt with a blanket wrapped around him in Josie Hunt's arms. Her legs felt like spaghetti, but she managed to walk up the steep incline. When she got to the top, she leaned against Dryden's pickup.

Josie carried Wyatt over.

"I'll take him." Zane held his hands out. As the investigator passed the child over to his grandpa, he stared up at the ranger.

Bliss's heart swelled. Suddenly, Chandler pulled up, and Sage exited the truck and ran their way.

"My baby." The mother burst into tears, and Wyatt leaped into her arms.

Zane took a step back to give her room.

Sage buried her face into Wyatt's neck. "I'm so glad to have you back."

A lump formed in Bliss's throat. No matter how many times she'd witnessed the reunion between child and parent, joy overwhelmed her. *Thank You, God, for bringing Wyatt home.*

"Daddy?"

Zane looked at his daughter.

"Thank you! I love you." She threw her arms around his neck. "I'm so sorry."

"Me too, honey."

Bliss stepped away to give them room and walked over to Josie, who moved beside her Bronco. "You did good."

The investigator cocked her head to one side. "Are you okay, boss?"

No, she wasn't okay. A complete emotional wreck was more like it. She was ecstatic Wyatt was rescued. And it looked like Sage and Zane might be on their way to mending their relationship.

Then why did she feel so alone?

But she gave her go-to answer. "I'm fine."

Josie searched her face. "You know, I've always respected you, but I must say, I wish you'd reconsider retiring from the Bring the Children Home Project. It will never be the same without you."

"I appreciate that." She turned around and saw that Zane was still talking with Sage. "Could you give me a ride back to my house? I'm exhausted."

"Sure. Do you need medical care?"

"No. Rest is what I want now." As she went to get in on the passenger side, she heard Zane calling her name. But she climbed inside anyway. She'd served her purpose.

Josie got in and shut the door. "The lieutenant is calling for you."

"I know. Please, let's go."

As they pulled away, she saw Zane in the side mirror watching them.

The truth was she'd miss him terribly. But she couldn't take another loss right now, especially a second time from the man she loved.

Zane's stomach twisted in knots as he stared after Josie's Bronco as it carried Bliss away.

Why had she left?

Had he done something wrong? Was she hurt?

Or was this like last time, when at a moment's notice, she decided she was joining the US Marshals. When he didn't immediately want her to leave, she had called off their wedding, caught a plane the same week and ignored his phone calls.

"Dad, I'm going back to the hotel to clean up. I'd like to visit with you later if that's all right."

"I'd like that." He gave Sage a hug and then scrubbed Wyatt on the head. "I'll see you later."

The boy smiled back.

Dryden strode over to Zane as he shoved his cell phone into his pocket. "Just talked to Captain Brewer. He's calling the governor to stop Sean Weaver's execution."

"Thanks. With the evidence, that shouldn't be a problem."

"Lieutenant, we've got some questions for you."

He turned to Officer Richards of the Liberty Police Department. No doubt their chief being involved in killing a cop and the attempted murders of several others was shocking. This mess would take a few hours to sort through, but he'd hoped to have Bliss at his side.

When Richards was done asking the questions, he looked at Zane like he was mulling something over in his head.

"What is it?" Zane asked.

"Chief Cunningham and I were rookies at the same time. He was always trying to make a name for himself."

"What are you saying?"

Richards shrugged. "I believe Cunningham was planting drugs at Sean Weaver's place so he could get the credit. I thought it was in jest, but Cunningham bragged back then he'd get his first big bust before any of us. Not only that, but the chief was always mouthing back then that once a user, always a user."

"Thanks, Richards."

Several hours later, he headed back to Liberty. Jason's truck had surfaced two miles downstream with him dead inside. Authorities were still looking for the driver of the white truck who worked with the chief. The vehicle was spotted on the east side of town near Peyton Fehan's known hangouts. Zane considered Officer Richards's comments. It made sense. Cunningham believed Sean was guilty of dealing drugs, so it wouldn't hurt to plant some at his house and get the credit for getting a dealer off the street. But he didn't know Officer Larson was already assigned to serve a search warrant at Weaver's place and would come through the door.

Bliss never left his mind. How could she have taken off without saying goodbye? He'd thought they were growing close again. Had he totally misread the situation?

Temptation to call and demand to know what was going on tugged at him. But he didn't want to start a disagreement. He never could've brought Wyatt home without her.

Frustration grew as he drove through Liberty and then to the outskirts of town. Wondering if Bliss had stopped by her office, he swung out of the way and drove by the Bring the Children Home Project. Josie's Bronco was the only vehicle in the parking lot. He pulled in.

When he walked through the glass door, Josie walked into the lobby.

"What can I do for you, Lieutenant?"

"Is Bliss here?"

Josie shook her head. "I'm sorry. She had me drop her off at her house."

He hated to involve others, especially one of the volunteers who worked with Bliss, but he was at a loss. "Was she hurt?"

She waved at him. "Come on back."

He followed her to her office.

"Would you like to take a seat?"

"I'll stand. Thanks." He had too much pent-up energy to sit.

"First, I've got to ask why Jason killed Larson and shot Weaver."

"It appears he was in the process of planting drugs at Weaver's place so that he could take him down and get the credit—trying to make a name for himself. He didn't know Larson was supposed to serve a search warrant. Larson must've interrupted him planting the drugs, and Cunningham panicked. Once he killed Larson, he shot Weaver and framed him for it."

"That makes sense." Josie leaned back in her chair and hesitated like she was considering her words. "I've worked for Bliss for several years, and she's a private person, as you probably know. I, along with the whole team, respect her." Josie made direct eye contact. "Might I suggest if you have anything you want to say to her, hunt her down and tell her."

He started to argue but held back.

"You know my boss doesn't like to talk about personal stuff. She mentioned once that she wanted to keep searching for her son no matter how many years he'd been missing. That there wasn't a worse feeling than not being worthy enough of someone coming after. I'm glad your grandson is safe now."

He stared at her for a moment, letting her comment sink in. "Thanks, Josie."

A slight smile came to her mouth. "You're welcome."

As he headed to his truck, he thought about it. Had she really believed he hadn't cared enough? He drove to her house, thinking about what he'd say to her.

What if she rejected him?

She was a chance he had to take.

When he pulled up to the gate, her voice came across the intercom. "What can I help you with, Lieutenant?"

"I need to talk with you."

"There's no need. I'm glad Wyatt is home now."

"Please, Bliss. Open the gate. One way or the other, I'm coming to talk to you. You're not running away from me this time."

After a few seconds, the gate opened, and he sped down the drive. When she opened the door, she didn't budge but stood there.

"May I come in?" Her mascara was smeared under her eyes, and she looked exhausted.

"Sure." She stood back and shut the door after him, and waited like she was expecting him to go into the living room.

Instead, he wrapped his arms around her waist and pulled her close. His gaze connected with hers. "I'm not letting you get away this time. I won't make that mistake again."

Her lips parted as if to protest, but he leaned down and kissed her. For a second, he thought she was going to kiss him back, but she pulled away.

"You don't have to—"

He planted his lips on her mouth again. This time, her arms moved around his neck, and she kissed him back.

When they parted, he kept his arms around her, enjoying being in her embrace again. "I love you, Bliss. Always have. I made some mistakes before and was hurt by your leaving. I should've come after you, but I was stupid and hurt. I'm not making that mistake again. If you don't like me, then I'll go. But if you like me even a little bit—" he held his fingers in a U shape "—give us another try."

A smile tugged at her mouth, and then seriousness returned before she stepped back. "What if I have nothing left to give?"

"We won't know until we try. One thing I've missed is having someone to lean on. You don't have to do everything yourself."

Her shoulders sagged. "Do you know how good those words are to hear? I love you, too. Always have." She wrapped her arms around his neck and gave him another kiss.

This time, he didn't let go of her for a long time.

EPILOGUE

One year later...

Bliss looked up as the back door slammed and Wyatt galloped into the room with Zane right behind him and Sugar yapping. "Grandpa said I'm not allowed to bring Ainsley in the house, but he let me feed her."

"I would think not. Skunks do not belong in the house. And Viv is sleeping." She held a finger to her lips, and then looked at the Maltese. "And that goes for you, too."

The white bundle of fur whined and put her head down.

"Sorry." Wyatt whispered so lightly he was difficult to understand.

She looked up at Zane and shook her head. "I can't believe you're allowing him to keep that skunk as a pet."

Zane strode over with a grin on his lips and kissed her on the top of her head. "I couldn't very well abandon the little thing since its mama disappeared." He glanced over her shoulder and slipped his finger into the nine-month-old baby's hand.

"Yeah," Wyatt joined in. "Even a skunk needs someone to take care of her."

Her husband's eyes glistened. "I'm amazed every time I look at Viv at how much she looks like Sage."

"She sent me a text earlier. She and John decided to do a little more shopping and asked if we mind watching the kids a little longer. I told her we'd be happy to."

A satisfied smile crossed his lips. "Good."

It was amazing how much Bliss's life had changed in the last year. She and Zane married ten months ago, just seven weeks after rescuing Wyatt, not wanting to put off their relationship any longer than necessary. Zane and Sage made amends almost immediately. His daughter admitted she'd been devastated when her mother was killed, and her dad was the easiest person to blame. But she'd been crushed when she left home at eighteen and he hadn't dragged her back home like she'd expected him to.

Viv's eyes slowly opened. She'd been awake all morning and had been ready for a nap. No doubt she was exhausted from all the playing. Bliss was enjoying being a grandma. Even though she was still running the Bring the Children Home Project, she allowed the others to help more. The team added three more volunteers and had managed to find two children three months ago who had been missing for over five years. The families would need a lot of counseling to deal with their ordeal, but they were on the right track.

Not all cases had a perfect ending, but the joy of knowing she did her part helped bring her fulfillment. Lawrence Weaver recovered from his injuries and lived to see his brother a free man. He died of liver cancer before his kidnapping case went to trial.

"Grandma, do you want to come see my skunk?" Wyatt tugged on her hand.

"I would love to." She smiled and climbed out of her chair, and Zane held his hands out for the baby.

"I'll take her." Viv smiled when her granddad took her.

As Bliss walked outside with Wyatt, she couldn't help but thank God for her family. Who would have thought the Texas lawman would be such a loving grandpa and husband? She truly was blessed.

* * * * *

If you liked this story from Connie Queen, check out her previous Love Inspired Suspense books:

Justice Undercover
Texas Christmas Revenge
Canyon Survival
Abduction Cold Case
Tracking the Tiny Target

Available now from Love Inspired Suspense!
Find more great reads at LoveInspired.com.

Dear Reader,

Thank you for reading Bliss and Zane's story.

Bliss's son had been missing for fourteen years, but it encouraged her to start the Bring the Children Home Project organization that assists law agencies in finding missing kids. After years of reuniting other children with their families, she learns her son won't be coming home.

I love happy endings, but stories about missing children tug at my heart. I can only imagine the feelings of loss and frustration. But for those who've lived this tragedy, may your community pull together and surround you in love, may the law agencies do their best to bring your child home, and most of all, I pray you find comfort and healing in the Lord.

I love to hear from readers! You can connect with me at www.conniequeenauthor.com or on my Facebook page.

Connie Queen

HARLEQUIN
PLUS

Try the best multimedia subscription service for romance readers like you!

Read, Watch and Play.

Experience the easiest way to get the romance content you crave.

Start your **FREE TRIAL** at
<u>www.harlequinplus.com/freetrial</u>.